THE CORNISH COLOURING BOOK CLUB

Beth Good

THIMBLERIG BOOKS

First published in 2017 by THIMBLERIG BOOKS,
Holsworthy, England

ISBN- 9781520938165

BETH GOOD

Beth Good was born and raised in Essex, England, then whisked away to an island tax haven at the age of eleven to attend an exclusive public school and rub shoulders with the rich and famous. Sadly, she never became rich or famous herself, so had to settle for infamy as a writer of dubious novels.

Starting out as an impoverished poet, Beth has been writing and publishing fiction since 1998, and no longer has to rely on a string of husbands to pay her bills. She writes both contemporary and historical fiction under various pseudonyms including Jane Holland, Victoria Lamb, Elizabeth Moss and Hannah Coates. Her work is both traditionally and independently published. Her latest publication as Jane Holland is a fast-paced psychological thriller: Girl Number One.

Beth currently lives in the West Country where she spends a great deal of time thinking romantic thoughts while staring out of her window at sheep. (These two activities are unrelated.)

For all my readers

**Other Publications by Jane Holland
writing as Beth Good**

Romantic Comedies

THE ODDEST LITTLE CHOCOLATE SHOP
THE ODDEST LITTLE CHRISTMAS SHOP
THE ODDEST LITTLE ROMANCE SHOP
THE ODDEST LITTLE BEACH SHOP
THE ODDEST LITTLE CHRISTMAS CAKE SHOP
THE ODDEST LITTLE BOOK SHOP
THE ODDEST LITTLE GINGERBREAD SHOP

Beth Good also writes novels as:

Jane Holland (thrillers)
Victoria Lamb (historical fiction)
Elizabeth Moss (romance)
Hannah Coates (feel-good fiction)

ACKNOWLEDGEMENTS

My grateful thanks to my readers, without whose enduring love and support I could not possibly keep writing as I do. So … keep the faith. This book is all your fault.

Beth x

CHAPTER ONE

I've made the biggest mistake of my life, Emma thought, and I've no idea how to fix it.

She was just reaching up to replace an encyclopaedia of Human Biology on the top shelf in the Reference section when this appalling realisation shot through her head.

At the same moment, a hand tugged twice on her flimsy summer dress and, much to Emma's relief, the unsettling thought fled. She was in the worst muddle ever. But she wasn't yet ready to face the consequences of what she'd done.

Startled, Emma turned. 'Yes?'

There was nobody there, which threw her for a second. On lowering her gaze to nearer knee-level though, she understood the problem.

'I need a wee-wee,' a small girl announced, and clutched meaningfully at her pale pink shorts. Her voice was high with desperation. 'Is there a toilet, please?'

'Of course,' Emma said swiftly, and took the little girl's hand. 'Where's your mummy? Or your daddy?'

'Mummy's in the toilet already. Changing my baby brother's nappy. She told me to stay and listen to the storyteller. Only now I need a wee too and I can't hang on.'

'Come on, I'll show you where.'

Emma led the hopping girl down the Reference section aisle with its huge books and thin foreign language pamphlets, and then threaded her way through a forest of empty buggies beside the children's section.

'It's not far,' she said reassuringly.

The girl nodded. 'Good.'

It was Stories For Under-Fives day at the library. There were usually at least twenty-five kids under five in attendance, most of them two and three-year-olds without full-time nursery placements, a few mere babes-in-arms.

The storytelling session was always lively, to say the least.

Emma was never sure what benefit the mothers felt it gave the very tiniest infants to sit and listen to the storyteller in the enclosed children's section of the library. Especially since most of the babies moaned and drooled and wailed their way through the two-hour session. The older kids enjoyed themselves though, clapping at more or less the right moments, and often joining in by guessing the next line of the story. So she supposed it didn't do the younger ones any harm to be brought along too.

Emma loved the peace and quiet of her job. But she didn't mind a bit of shouting out and children's laughter now and then. The library could be too quiet at times. And right now, she was keen to be distracted from the tangled complexity of her thoughts.

The little girl's mother was Carmen, a loud and demonstrative woman she knew as a regular attendee of the under-fives storytelling sessions. She was dragging a buggy backwards out of the toilets as Emma approached, looking flustered, a high colour in her cheeks.

Carmen caught sight of her daughter and exclaimed rather crossly, 'Siobhan? Why have you left the others? I told you – '

'She needs the toilet,' Emma explained.

'Oh, Siobhan.'

'Here,' she said quickly, seeing the little girl's lip begin to tremble and fearing an accident, 'let me help. I'll mind Baby while you take her into the toilets.' She smiled when the woman began to protest that she must be too busy. 'No, really, Carmen, it's no trouble.'

So Emma stood patiently by the buggy while the mother escorted her little girl back into the toilets. The baby boy looked up at her speculatively, then blew a series of bubbles with his own saliva. It was not an entirely attractive process to watch.

Normally she would have pulled a face and looked away. Today though, Emma found herself staring at the child, suddenly fascinated.

'Oh my God, have you stolen a baby?'

She turned at the joke, flustered and ridiculously guilty. 'Ha ha, very funny.'

It was Harold, one of the other librarians, who had come sneaking up on her while she was admiring the baby.

Harold was a little younger than her but had got himself a PhD, so was actually her senior at work. His dark curly hair seemed to cover much of his face as well as his head, not helped by a generous beard and sideburns, so that Emma always instinctively thought of him as 'hirsute Harold'. Like some character out of an Old Testament story.

He grinned down at the baby. 'Seriously, whose kid is it?'

'Carmen. The one who complained the other week.'

'I remember Carmen.'

Emma indicated the toilets with her head. 'She'll be out in a minute. I said I'd watch him for her.'

'So who's watching the front desk?'

'Mr Nobody.' She shrugged at his annoyed expression. 'What? It's all automated these days. Bleep them in, bleep them out.'

'There's meant to be someone on hand for queries,' Harold pointed out, but mildly, with an air of faint disappointment, as though she was a favourite child who had broken a long-held rule. 'A human presence. You know that.'

'What's more human than helping out a harassed mum?'

Before Harold could formulate an adequate response, the toilet door swung open and Siobhan came out, still adjusting her shorts.

'Thank you,' she piped to Emma, and trotted past on her way back to the story session.

Her mother followed her, taking charge of the buggy again. 'Thank you,' Carmen said, and smiled indulgently down at her baby.

Emma's eyes widened. She had the impression the mother was doing a quick inventory of her child's fingers and toes, as though worried someone might have swiped some while her back was turned.

'Mummy's back now. Did you miss me? Aw, did my ickle man miss his mumsy-wumsy? Ooh, that's a lovely big bubble.' Carmen jerked the buggy into violent motion, and the baby's head swayed perilously back and forth. She could give him whiplash doing that, Emma thought. 'Come on, Trevor, let's see what your big sister is up to.'

Trevor?

Once the woman was safely out of earshot, Harold grinned at her. 'That's a good, old-fashioned name.'

'Maybe it's after his granddad. Anyway, you can't talk. What was your mother's excuse?'

Harold shrugged, but looked taken aback by the question. 'I was named after my maternal grandfather,' he agreed, then frowned at her. 'You seem out of sorts. Everything okay?'

Their eyes met.

Suddenly she was tempted to say no. To blurt everything out to Harold, of all people. It was a moment of sheer, blundering panic.

Then, thankfully, mercifully, like the abrupt righting of a capsized boat, common sense reasserted itself.

She could not tell *anyone*. Least of all a work colleague.

'Yes, everything's fine, no worries at all.' Somehow Emma dredged up a smile from the depths, though she knew her eyes must surely betray her. 'I was miles away, that's all. Thinking about this club I've set up.'

'The colouring book club? For adults?'

'I put a small ad in the newspaper, like you suggested, and I've plastered the lobby and the main notice board with posters. Plus, I've booked the upstairs meeting room for Monday evening. Only now I'm a little bit worried nobody will turn up.' She gave him a crooked smile. 'That I'll end up sitting all by myself for two hours, colouring away on my own like a total muppet.'

'You want me to come too? To keep you company?'

'Oh gosh, that's very kind of you.' Emma paused, not sure what to say. She knew Harold had some kind of extra-curricular interest in her. But she had none whatsoever in him. It would be wrong to encourage him too far along that path just to save her ego from an embarrassing knock. 'But no, I don't think you need to make the ultimate sacrifice.'

Harold grinned.

She added, 'I'm probably just being silly. The event is on the library Facebook page, and there are a few posters up around town too. I expect someone will turn up.'

'I can share the details on my own Facebook page, if you like.'

'That'd be very helpful, thanks.'

Harold only had a few dozen friends on Facebook, and she was fairly sure none of them would be interested in colouring books for adults. He was a sci-fi fanatic who shared movie posters and interviews with science fiction writers on Facebook.

But it was a nice gesture.

Harold was still studying her though, his head on one side. 'You sure there's nothing wrong, Emma?'

'Bit of a headache, that's all.'

'I hate headaches. They're the worst. You need some time off. Or more time off, I should say. Perhaps you're missing the dance vibes of Ibiza?' He nudged her, awkward in his chumminess. 'You never did say how your holiday went. Not one for clubbing myself, but whatever turns you on. I expect the island's quite attractive in early summer too.'

Somehow Emma maintained her smile, miraculously. She gestured to the toilets without responding to his question.

'Do you mind?'

Harold looked surprised. But he stammered something and disappeared on cue. She didn't like having to be mean to Harold, he was one of the few friends she had at work. But if there was one thing she absolutely did not want to discuss with anyone, let alone her colleagues at the library, it was her bloody holiday in Ibiza.

To her relief, there was no one in the ladies.

On her way to her favourite toilet cubicle, Emma paused to check herself in the mirrors above the row of sinks.

A little pale this morning, but otherwise much the same as ever, elbow-length chestnut hair – her crowning glory, according to her very middle-class mother and father – piled up in an impressive bun, a few wisps allowed to escape for effect, the merest hint of foundation and a soft pearlescent pink lipstick to add a little colour. Summer dress, but knee-length, muted colours, no jewellery. Nicely rounded chest, large hips, a figure heading without too much regret from a UK size fourteen to a sixteen.

In short, Emma looked like exactly what she was.

A well turned-out professional woman, nearly thirty, comfortably built, single – and ever so slightly, ever so secretly, pregnant.

CHAPTER TWO

'Many happy returns, darling.'

'Sorry?'

Crystal straightened, and looked round at her mother in surprise.

'Oh dear. That is, I meant to say,' her mother was floundering now, her eyes wide, 'Happy Birthday.'

'Thanks.'

'I do wish you many happy returns though. And I'm sure you'll get them, and they'll be very happy.'

'Really, it's fine, mum. Forget about it.'

Crystal smiled, and bent down again to continue with her task of tidying the inside of their beach hut. She did not know how it had got into such a mess when they hardly ever came up here, deckchairs, sun umbrellas and windbreaks all jumbled together.

But she was interrupted again as her smart phone buzzed in her pocket.

Her heart beat a little faster.

Crystal fished out her phone and glanced swiftly down at the screen.

It was nothing exciting.

One of her recent retweets had been retweeted again,

that was all. Some charity link for an upcoming event at a local coffee shop that she probably wouldn't be able to attend because she had a doctor's appointment that day. She ought to turn off her Twitter notifications. They were never desperately interesting these days.

Surreptitiously, she checked her Facebook page for the third time that hour, but there was nothing new there either.

No birthday messages from her old boss or any of her mates from the London office. Not even from Taylor, a guy she'd dated briefly at Christmas and still considered a friend.

What on earth had she expected though?

It was over a month since she'd given up her job in the city and moved back to the remote depths of Cornwall. Those guys had better things to do than keep in touch with a former colleague. Especially one in her precarious situation.

Out of sight, out of mind.

'Remind me, darling,' her mother said, interrupting her self-pity fest, 'how old are you this birthday?'

Crystal stared round at her. 'Sorry?' she repeated.

'Things like that slip my mind these days. Only to be expected, isn't it? I'm not exactly old but I'm not exactly young either. Besides,' her mother added ruminatively, 'maths was never my strong point.'

She couldn't argue with that. Crystal turned off her smartphone before the continuing lack of Facebook notifications could drive her any deeper into gloom.

'I'm twenty-five, mum.'

'My goodness, are you absolutely sure?'

'Pretty much.'

'Well, I suppose you must know your own age. Though I can hardly believe it's possible. I have a child who's twenty-five years old.' Her mother lowered the romantic novel she had been reading ever since they arrived at the beach hut, and looked out at the looming swell of the

Atlantic. 'Time is a funny old thing, isn't it?'

Since it was not a question that demanded an answer, Crystal let it sink into the sunny air without response.

The top tier of beach huts was new that summer. As locals, they had been lucky to get first dabs on one of the spacious end huts overlooking the popular Cornish bay before they were all snatched up by wealthy second home owners. She gazed down at the golden sands below. The beach was surprisingly quiet, given the summer season was in full swing. She watched the tide slowly wash in amongst tiny inlets and rock pools on its mission to fill the whole bay.

A charming vista, the beach hut agent had said. And it was.

Her mum was right. It had been a good idea to sit beside the sea on her birthday. Gloom had enveloped her yet again when she rolled out of bed this morning, the bleak tinge of pessimism that was always at the back of her mind these days, creeping back in, refusing to go away. But in this brilliant sunshine, even that gloom might be beatable.

Just about.

'Take me,' her mum continued, sniffing at the salt-drenched air. 'Nearly twice your age, yet I feel seventeen in my head.'

Still act it too, Crystal thought, but gave her mum a smile. She meant well.

There was a sudden sharp gust from the Atlantic. It blew her skirt right up over her back, and sent the hut door swinging violently towards her legs.

Startled, Crystal thrust the door open again with a firm hand, and dragged down her skirt with the other. 'Damn thing.'

'Oh, do be careful.' Her mother sat up, sounding concerned for her. Yet again. 'What on earth are you doing over there?'

'Showing off my knickers.'

'Well, why don't you leave that for another day and sit next to me? The view is stunning. Really stunning. Besides, you shouldn't be over-exerting yourself.'

Chance would be a fine thing, Crystal thought wryly, but said nothing. Recently, her mother had started to complain every time she tried to do anything more strenuous than taking out the bins.

'Please come and sit down, love,' her mother said again, and patted the deckchair next to her. 'You're making me nervous.'

There was no point arguing with her mother. Not today, of all days.

Crystal gave up on her tidying, fastened the beach hut door shut against any more sudden whipping of the breeze, and sat next to her mother.

My special day, she thought ironically, and shifted in her seat. The blue-and-white striped deckchair was not uncomfortable. But if she sat here too long, her back would ache. Perhaps they ought to have brought cushions as well as a packed lunch.

The sea view really was very impressive, she had to admit. But she loved the colourful row of beach huts too. Their beach hut was made of white wooden slats that reflected the sun, the door the same bright red as the cherry tomatoes in their packed lunch. She preferred that shade to the mustard-yellow door next along to them, and the lettuce-green after that. Red was such a vibrant colour. The colour of life and vitality. Not to mention tomatoes. Then Crystal thought of blood, and remembered that red was also the colour of death.

Not a particularly cheery thought for her birthday.

'Anyway, here you go,' her mum said brightly. She fished in her beach bag and produced a well-wrapped present. 'Happy Birthday. Something to take your mind off your troubles.'

'I said you didn't need to get me anything for my birthday.'

'I know, I know. And I ignored you, as always.' Her mum nodded at the present, looking impatient. 'Go on, open it.'

Crystal tore off the wrapping paper, and stared in surprise at a large white paperback book and a packet of felt-tip pens. The book featured the outline of a crowded jungle scene on the cover, attractive enough but entirely colourless. As in, without colour.

Bemused, she read the book title aloud, '*Jungle Galore: A Colouring Book for Adults*,' then turned to stare at her mother. 'I'm sorry. A *what* for *who*?'

'Colouring books for adults. They're all the rage at the moment.'

'It's very kind of you, Mum. But a colouring book?' Crystal was trying hard not to laugh. 'Not my thing, I'm afraid.'

'Fair enough.' Her mum leant over, removed the book from her grasp, and flicked through a few pages. She smiled. 'Oh, look at that lion. He's very majestic. And all these flamingos. So exotic. Do they really only have one leg, or are they just bending them out of … Oh, I see.' She paused in her restless flicking, and frowned over another page. 'Goodness me. Is that a python?'

'I'm not taking up colouring, Mum.'

'Very well, if you're not interested, that's no problem. No need to waste my present. I'll just have a go myself. I believe colouring is a very calming hobby.'

Her mum closed the book and folded both hands over it, almost protectively. She looked out to sea, a thoughtful expression on her face.

'So tell me, Crystal, what are you planning to do with yourself this summer? Start surfing again? Learn to jet-ski, maybe?' she asked, her voice deceptively unemotional. 'Remind me, why did you give up your high-powered job in London and come home to Cornwall?'

'Don't.'

'Perhaps you should take up rock climbing instead.'

Her mum nodded towards the cliff on the other side of the bay. Its jagged peaks were a dark, muscular granite, topped with grassy turf that looked almost luminous in the sunlight. 'No problem for someone with your athletic prowess. Bet you could scale that cliff in ten minutes, once you'd got the hang of it.'

Crystal shook her head. She stared out at the sea for a few moments in a stony silence. Then held out her hand for the colouring book.

'Fine, let me have the colouring book.'

'You won't regret it.'

'I already regret it.' Listlessly, Crystal flicked through the colouring book and stopped on a page at random. It featured some kind of giant frog or toad – she wasn't sure which, but it had a bumpy back – surrounded by leafy jungle fronds. 'Pens?'

Her mother handed over the packet of felt-tips, smiling.

'I just hope there are plenty of greens in here,' Crystal added. 'Because I'm going to need at least three different shades.'

'That's the spirit.'

Crystal hooked out a dark green felt-tip in a shade that reminded her of boiled spinach, and set to work on a frond. It was more intricate work than she had expected. She frowned, focusing on the spiky outline so she would not go over the lines, then began to wonder what colour the toad ought to be. Of course, it was entirely up to her. She could make it a blue toad if she wanted. Or a bright neon pink one. Assuming there was a pen that colour in the pack.

After a few minutes, to her surprise, she realised that she had become quite absorbed by the task of colouring. Having to focus on not making a mess of the picture had taken her mind off her recent gloominess.

Automatically, she started checking for other fronds in the picture that could be coloured with the same dark green pen.

'I'm told it's an excellent activity for balancing your chakras,' her mother said softly, watching her.

'There's nothing wrong with my chakras,' Crystal said tartly, always impatient with her mother's eccentric beliefs. Then regretted her tone when her mum sighed and looked away out to sea. Her mother was only trying to help. In her own peculiar way. 'But you're right, it is strangely calming, I have to admit. And it does give me something to do with my hands that isn't, you know, *knitting*.'

Her mum said nothing, her gaze still fixed on the thin blue line of the horizon. 'I could do with balancing my chakras.'

The sea was a warm indigo, brushed with brisk white rollers that curled in off the Atlantic Ocean at regular intervals. The waves were not powerful enough for surfing today. She could see a few determined body-boarders out there in the water though, black dots of wetsuits that rose and fell with the tide, their heads glistening like seals.

'Sounds painful.'

'Since the divorce, things have been tight. Money-wise, you know. If your bloody father had let me have his share of the business … But oh no, *Dick* made me buy him out.' She said his name with pointed significance. 'That took the last of my savings, you know. So if the guesthouse goes bump, I'll be broke. I've sunk everything in it.'

'Mum, that's not going to happen.' Crystal gave her a quick reassuring smile. 'I know suddenly landing on you like this from London has given you an extra mouth to feed. I'm really sorry about that. And I'm going to help out where I can.'

'In your condition?'

Crystal pulled a face. 'Good grief. My condition? You make me sound … pregnant.'

'Oh God, don't even go there. That would be the cherry on the cake.' Her mum shook her head. She was looking tired and depressed, Crystal thought. Which was not surprising, given the state of both their lives this year. 'Perhaps we should head back to the guesthouse. What if there's been a delivery that needed a signature? Or one of tonight's guests has turned up early and the place is deserted?'

Having finished colouring in all the larger fronds, Crystal snapped the lid back on the dark green pen and rooted in the packet for a lighter green.

There was only a pale lime green. Not ideal, but what choice did she have if she wanted to finish the picture?

'Mum, we came to the beach hut today so we could chill out together for a few hours. Not worry about all the little things that could be going wrong in your absence.'

'True.'

Crystal began to colour in the smaller fronds with the lime-green felt tip, trying to sound more optimistic than she was. 'Anyway, my condition is not going to stop me being a help this summer. I may not be up to jet-skiing, it's true. But I'm perfectly able to cook and clean, and change the occasional bed. Everything's going to be okay.'

Her mother sounded a little reassured. 'You really believe that?'

No, Crystal thought, but said aloud, 'Of course.'

'Oh, well.'

Her mother gave a contented noise under her breath and turned back to stare at the sea.

Crystal glanced that way too. The warm sunshine had started to bring out the tourists after a week of unseasonably cool weather. Below them on the sands, the surf school was in full swing, instructors leading would-be surfers down to the water's edge with surf boards carried above their heads. And the beachside café was doing steady business too, several people queuing for ice creams at the window hatch. The place was under new management since she had last been here. Crystal could see the owner's son wiping down the outside tables, a hulking fair-haired guy in cut-off denims. Attractive enough, but not her type.

Too old for me, she thought, guessing him to be about thirty. Though it might be fun to date someone older for once. And thirty was not *that* old.

Crystal had been smiling as she reached for a new felt tip, but abruptly the smile failed. She could hardly think about dating, even if he had been her type. Not anymore.

'Hey, look at this. A new book club. And local too.' Her mum ringed something in the local paper, and shoved the newspaper under her nose. 'I think you should go, Crystal. We could both go, in fact.'

'Hold on, let me read it first.'

'Now, darling, don't go all stroppy on me – '

'Colouring Book Club, to meet monthly,' Crystal began to read out, and then shook her head vehemently. 'Oh no, no way. Colouring, yes. I accept that colouring-in is not as stupid as I thought. It is rather soothing, I'll give you that. But go to a monthly book club for people who like colouring? Are you kidding?' She handed back the newspaper. 'What do they even do there? Sit around and colour together?'

'I don't know. But we'll find out if we go, won't we?'

'I'm not a joiner. I hate groups. Besides, they sound like a bunch of muppets.'

'One time only? Just to see what it's like?'

'Mum –'

'Please.' Her mum took off her sunglasses and did the sad, squashed cabbage face she reserved for really special favours. 'Pleeeeease.'

'You don't even like colouring books. You only got this one to torture me.'

'I need a new hobby. And so do you. To keep your mind off …' Her mum made a face, and did not continue with that difficult thought. Instead, she added lightly, 'Colouring is perfect for you. No physical activity involved. Anyone can do it.'

'Anyone with plenty of felt tips and no brain cells.'

Her mum put her sunglasses back on, smiling benignly. 'We'll buy more.'

'You can buy brain cells?'

'Felt tips.'

'Oh God, tell me you're not serious about this.'

'You'll love it.'

Crystal buried her face in her hands, groaning.

'I knew you'd see sense.' Her mum read the newspaper ad through again. 'First meeting is next Monday evening at the library. That's brilliant, there's no clash. Not even with my knitting circle. And young Patrick from next door can earn a few quid by minding the guesthouse while we're out.'

'He'll burn the place down in five minutes.'

Her mother gave her a hard, sideways stare. 'Now listen, you said everything was going to be *okay*,' she reminded her, her tone accusing.

Crystal watched one determined woman in a wetsuit striding out through the surf, a neon-blue body board under her arm despite the lack of waves today. Perhaps she needed to cool down though. The summer sunshine was getting a little too hot now, and the blue water of the Atlantic looked inviting.

It was pointless to keep resisting her mother over this crazy idea. The tide would come rushing in every time, regardless of whatever barriers she put up against it.

'You'll need to buy another colouring book if we both go to this meeting,' Crystal pointed out.

She bent her head again, beginning to colour the toad a deep, rusty red. It looked startlingly impressive beside the dark green fronds. Perhaps it would not be so bad to go to a colouring book club. She could get into this hobby, given its peaceful and non-energetic nature, and there might be some other interesting colouring books on offer there.

'For yourself,' she added. 'You can't share mine, it's impractical.'

'We'll need several more books,' Fiona agreed. 'But

don't worry, I can easily get them online. Let's see, it's Wednesday today. If I order them tonight, they should arrive in good time for Monday.'

'Got it all worked out, haven't you?'

Her mother tilted her head back and basked in the sunlight. There were a few silver strands among the red hair they both shared, her mother's worn long and loose, her own cut short to the neck.

'You're my only daughter, Crystal, and you've come home in trouble.' There was a deep note of satisfaction in her mother's voice, Crystal thought, and something else too. Something sweet and wholly unexpected. Something that made tears prick at her eyes. 'I'm going to take care of you.'

CHAPTER THREE

Pregnant.

Emma stared at herself in the mirror above the sinks, still hoping this was might turn out to be a bad dream. But no, the image did not change. She was wide awake and at work in the library, and her nightmare was still true. She was expecting a baby.

Fear rippled through her like nausea. Real nausea followed in its wake, already familiar from her early morning visits to the bathroom. She clutched the cold rim of the sink, bent her head, and breathed slow and shallow, trying not to panic.

This morning, she had finally given in to her suspicions and done a pregnancy test, worried now that her period was a few weeks late – yet still not quite believing it could be possible.

The thin pink line had shocked her with its irrefutable reality.

Pregnant.

'One night.' She raised her head, looking at herself accusingly in the mirror. 'One bloody stupid night.'

Of course, she knew what her mother and father would say. Getting rid of the pregnancy was the only sensible course open to her.

Emma was unmarried, they would point out, entirely without irony, and renting a one-bedroom apartment in a house of similar self-contained flats. A bedsit, in other words. Her career was gaining momentum. Her salary was not brilliant, but it was enough for a single person, and she was finally paying off her student loans. Another few years, she should have enough for a deposit on a first home.

Most importantly, she did not have a relationship with the baby's father. Not even remotely. The brutal truth was that she did not know his name. Nor where he lived. All she knew for sure was that he was English and a little older than her and irresistibly sexy.

It had been one night in Ibiza, that was all.

One wild, crazy night on the sands in the arms of a stranger.

One night led astray by the beguiling smile of a rave DJ with all-over tattoos and a surprisingly hot ponytail.

Her mind had been in a different space that night in Ibiza. Whirling with music, high on mellow vibrations, open to strange new friendships, to life and the universe. No time for realism. No sobering thoughts of protection, of potential consequences. She recalled warm sands, kisses in the darkness, neon lights reflected in the rippling water, the thump-thump-thump of a distant beat …

One night, that was all.

One mistake.

And this tiny life in her womb was the result of her mistake.

She had to get to the doctor. And she would do. As soon as she could arrange for an appointment. To talk logistics. Discuss dates.

Get rid of it.

Even as those words came into her head, that disturbing phrase, *get rid of it*, Emma knew it was impossible. Having a baby was impossible, yes, absolutely. But getting rid of her unwanted child was every damn bit as impossible.

One huge and wholly unexpected complication.

Two equally grim solutions.

And here she was, single and on the cusp of thirty, trapped in a cage of her own making, staring at herself in the mirror as if her eyes might hold the key.

What on earth was she to do?

Her smartphone buzzed in the wide pocket of her dress. Emma fumbled for it, stared blindly at the screen. Someone wanting to be her friend on Facebook. She checked the name, her heart beating hard. But it was just one of the women from the monthly book club she sometimes attended. Not a very exciting club, she always ended up listening to one very opinionated person and not daring to say she disagreed with her.

Which was one reason she had decided to set up a colouring book club. So everyone could participate equally. Not to mention the relaxation part. Nothing more relaxing after a long day at work than listening to soft music while colouring in a lovely picture.

Out of habit, she checked her emails.

Nothing.

It was a half-chance. At some point during that barely-recalled evening of discarded inhibitions, she had scribbled her email down on a torn-out scrap of magazine paper and handed it to him. To whatever his name was. The anonymous stranger who had astonishingly managed to impregnate her and then disappear forever.

Had he told her his name?

Yes, she had a vague memory of …

But every time Emma tried to remember the name he had whispered in her ear that night, the memory ebbed away like smoke, like a tide on the turn.

How on earth was she supposed to find an Englishman she had known on holiday for only a few hours and whose name she could not remember, let alone where he lived?

It felt hopeless. She was alone in a deep pit of her

own digging. What she desperately needed was something – or someone – to pull her out.

But who?

Crystal must have fallen asleep in her deckchair, because the sun was much higher when she woke up. Her legs were a bit numb and she had a crick in her neck. Frowning at the brightness of the sun, she dabbed blindly at her mouth, suddenly and horribly aware that she had been drooling.

'Excuse me?'

Yes, that was what had woken her. A man's voice, cutting through the background noise of rolling waves and people on the beach.

Oh God.

She sat up, flushed and disorientated, looking about for her mother.

The deckchair next to her was empty.

Typical.

She had been deserted by her mother, probably as soon as her eyelids had closed. No doubt Fiona had seen that Crystal was asleep and slipped away for one of her brisk walks, or maybe for a coffee at the beach café.

A shadow fell over her face as she turned round, surreptitiously wiping away any last traces of drool.

The man who had spoken was younger than his voice sounded, she realised. About her own age, mid-twenties.

And bloody gorgeous.

Dark hair, smiling dark eyes, a bit on the skinny side, dressed casually in trainers, grey jeans and a tight black T-shirt that showed off his pecs and flat abs rather excellently. To her relief, there was none of that self-conscious vanity in his face, the kind she associated with men who were athletic-looking and physically attractive, and knew it. Men like her last boyfriend, Taylor, who had wasted no time in disappearing when she admitted to not being one hundred percent fit.

'Sorry,' the guy was saying, holding up a hammer.

For one wild moment, Crystal thought he was a crazed beach hut murderer, come to bash her cranium in while she dozed in her deckchair. She stiffened in shock.

But he lowered the hammer again, grinning at her expression. 'My granddad's hut door isn't shutting properly. Number fifty-seven. The council said it might take a few days to send someone out here to fix it. So I've come to give it a whack myself.'

She frowned, still not understanding.

'I saw you were asleep, so thought I'd better try to wake you up before I started making a racket.' He hesitated. 'It's right next door here. You don't mind, do you?'

'Of course not.'

He studied her face, then leant forward with his left hand. 'Perhaps I'd better start again, I think you may have been asleep through some of that explanation. Hi, I'm Jack.'

Jack.

It suited him. Straightforward, fun, easy-going. Maybe a bit of a ladies' man. Not to be taken too seriously, she thought.

'No, I heard you just fine.' Awkwardly, she shook his left hand. Or waved it up and down, as he was still holding a hammer in his right hand. 'I'm Crystal.'

His eyes widened. 'Wow.'

'I know.'

She threw aside the colouring book on her lap, and pushed impatiently out of the deckchair. Her legs felt stiff after sitting so long, but she persevered. She did not want him to think she was a total sloth.

'My mum's a bit of a hippy,' she added, by way of explanation.

'No, I love it.'

Jack had such sexy eyes, she found herself staring at him. At his face. His easy, slightly crooked smile. Stubble on his jaw. He was really very yummy.

'Thanks.'

'I don't want to be rude, but I don't know you,' he said bluntly. 'I know most people my age round here.' He glanced briefly at her summer skirt and strappy vest top. 'Are you on holiday?'

'No, I live here. Now.'

'Ah.'

'That is, I didn't go to school here. Mum moved down from London about five years ago, to open a guesthouse. I came with her, but then went back to London after a while. To work, you know.' She grimaced. 'I love Cornwall. It's a really special place. But a bit too quiet for me out of season.'

'You've come back though.'

'Just recently.'

'For good?"

His dark eyes were intent on her face. She floundered about for an answer, finding his close stare a little disconcerting.

'Hard to tell.'

His nod was brisk. As though he had come to the end of his interest in her. 'Well, sorry to have woken you up. But I promised the old fella I'd come by today, see if I can't sort out this door for him.'

There were pens scattered under her deckchair, she realised, seeing his glance. Her felt tips. She bent to gather them together. How embarrassing.

'I can't believe I fell asleep.'

He shrugged, turning to survey the next door beach. The one with the number fifty-seven above a mustard yellow door. 'Sea air, all this warm sun. I'd fall asleep myself if I wasn't permanently on my feet.'

Crystal laughed.

He looked at the felt tip pens. 'Like drawing, do you?'

'It's for a colouring book.'

Jack smiled. 'Oh, one of them.'

'My mum's idea. Not mine. She thinks I need

something to do. Can't stand to see people idle.'

'Sounds like a sensible woman.'

'You haven't met her. Pick the furthest point from sensible, and that's my mother. She only handed me one of those books for the first time today, and already she's trying to drag me along to some local colouring-in club she spotted in the newspaper.'

'Not going to happen?'

She shrugged, reluctant to look foolish in front of this good-looking stranger but equally unhappy about making it sound like she didn't get on with her darling mum.

'I suppose it might be worth a look.'

'Everything's worth a look.' He smiled. 'Well, I hope you two have a good time at your club.'

'Not your kind of thing either, I take it?'

'I think it would probably depend who else was there,' he replied after a long pause, and then distinctly winked at her.

She did not know what to say to that.

Jack leant the hammer against the hut wall and fished a key out of his jeans pocket. He unlocked the door of beach hut number fifty-seven, then stood there a moment, head down, examining the door hinges with tremendous attention.

She thought of the bearded old man whom she had occasionally seen sitting outside the beach hut, smoking a pipe and staring at the ocean with a faraway look in his eyes. She could see a certain family resemblance, she thought. Though of course it was hard to tell for sure, given the old man's bushy beard and thick, slightly wild grey eyebrows.

'Old Thomas is your granddad?'

'Hard to believe? It's the beard, right? Because I don't have one?'

'No, honestly. I was just –'

'Making conversation? Chatting me up?' Jack grinned over his shoulder at her when she fell silent. 'Don't look so worried, I'm only kidding.'

She did not know what to say. Or where to look. He had a very engaging smile.

Too bloody engaging.

There were footsteps on the path up from the seafront. The steady slap of flip-flops. Crystal turned, relieved to see her mother coming back up the steep incline, arms swinging, her face a little flushed from the sun. Fiona was forty-three now, but kept herself fit and active, not just through running the guesthouse but doing sports with her friends whenever she could. She even ran the occasional ten kilometre race for charity. And Crystal herself had always enjoyed sports. Which made it all the more ironic now that she found even the slightest activity tiring, and had to rest even when walking *downhill* these days.

'Oh, you're awake,' her mum said, then stared at the young man. 'Hello.'

'This is Jack,' Crystal said quickly. Too quickly, her voice suspiciously high. As though she found him attractive and was somehow embarrassed. Which was utterly ridiculous. She stuffed the errant felt tips back into the plastic pack. 'He's old Thomas' grandson. Come to fix that dodgy door at last.'

Her mum smiled at him cheerfully, patting her sweaty forehead with a tissue. 'Hullo, I'm Fiona. Though I prefer Fifi. Makes me feel younger.'

'Younger than what?'

'Methuselah.'

'Good to meet you, Fifi. You don't look so old to me.'

'Oh, I like you,' her mum said with a wink, then added brightly, 'Did Crystal tell you? It's her birthday today. She's twenty-five.'

He looked round at her. 'Happy Birthday.'

Slowly, Crystal felt herself grow warm under his scrutiny.

'Thanks.'

Her mum's gaze narrowed on her face too. 'Darling,

you look awfully pink. Have you caught the sun?'

Crystal glared at her, speechless.

'Maybe I shouldn't have left you as long as I did. But the view was too gorgeous to resist, so I popped down for a walk along the beach while the tide was out. It's lovely down there, the sea breeze cooled me right down. I didn't think you'd wake up so soon.' Fiona bent and retrieved her things, then began folding up her deckchair. 'Shall we go?'

They packed up the beach hut and locked it again. Crystal glanced over her shoulder as they walked down the winding, grassy path to the seafront, and was surprised to see Jack leaning against the mustard yellow door, watching her. Like he was *interested*. Which was impossible. Not after catching her drooling in a deckchair like some octogenarian, a colouring book open on her lap, felt tips scattered all over the place.

And even if he was, it wasn't something she could ever encourage.

Not in her 'condition'.

'That Jack looks like a nice lad.' Her mum shot a sideways glance at her face. 'Don't you agree?'

'Hardly a lad.'

'I wonder if he's into colouring books. Or fish and chip suppers. They do a nice piece of haddock at the beach café.' Fiona looked bemused when Crystal thumped her arm. 'Ow, what was that for?'

'For being the world's most infuriating matchmaker. Now shut up. You know I can't date anyone. Not right now.'

'Why can't you?' her mum asked, stubborn as ever.

'Because I could be dead soon.'

CHAPTER FOUR

Crystal stopped at the entrance doors to the library. It was time. In fact, they were running late. They needed to go inside. She knew that. But she looked round at her mother instead.

'I'm not sure about this, Mum. A colouring book club. It sounds awful. And I don't even know anyone older than ten who enjoys colouring in other people's pictures – except you, of course. What if I hate it? What if all the people there are weird?' She paused, frowning. 'Weirder than us, that is.'

'Oh, get inside with you.' Fiona shoved her in the back, albeit gently and with understanding. 'Go on, enough of that nonsense. You were exactly the same back when you started primary school. *What if I don't like the teachers? What if I don't enjoy finger-painting?*' Fiona shook her head. 'We only get one life, Crystal. You need to start living yours.'

Crystal hated her mum.

She loved her too, of course. Fiercely and without compromise.

But oh goodness, Fiona could be annoying.

They were in the broad lobby of the library, all glass and stone-coloured floor tiles. Dead ahead on the wall was a hand-drawn poster for the club.

COLOURING BOOK CLUB, the poster proclaimed, along with all the club details.

There was an impressive attempt at ornate calligraphy on the poster too, vivid reds and blues adorning the insides of the Os and Bs.

'There,' Fiona said, suddenly jabbing the air with her finger. 'It says we're meeting in the upstairs reading room. Shall we go straight up? Or do you want to browse the library first?'

Crystal checked the time on her phone. 'Bit late for browsing, Mum. We'd better get straight to the meeting. I don't want to be the last person through the door.'

They were heading up the stairs when a cheerful voice hailed them from behind, making Fiona jump.

'Hello again, ladies.'

They both looked round. It was the man from the beach huts. The good-looking one with the big hammer.

'You,' Crystal stammered.

'Me,' he agreed without any display of surprise, and held out his hand. 'I'm Jack. Remember?'

Her mum was looking delighted. 'Of course we remember you, Jack. From the beach. How lovely to see you again.' She glanced from his face to Crystal's, then back again, her smile like a Cheshire cat's. It was not hard to guess what she was thinking. 'Are you here for the colouring club too?'

'That's right.'

Crystal stared. 'Seriously?'

'Why not?'

He held up a packet of pens and a colouring book. The pens looked brand-new, still unopened in their plastic pack. The book was pristine too. There was a swirling Eastern mandala on the front, all complicated loops and squares and circles.

Very restful, no doubt, Crystal thought, gazing at the intriguing designs. She was not sure about the owner though. This had the air of a planned encounter. Jack had not been that keen on colouring when she mentioned it to him on the beach. In fact, she had got the impression that he thought it a waste of time.

'Perhaps you think only women like colouring books?' Jack added, and raised his eyebrows in a challenging way.

She did not know what to say, so shrugged helplessly.

But her brain was whirring.

Could Jack have come to the library tonight just to meet her again? An impossible thought. Yet here he was.

Minus his hammer.

Which was probably a good thing, as otherwise she might have been tempted to use it on him. Or on her match-making mother.

'Well, you can come along with us,' Fiona was saying with a broad smile, her gesture inclusive. She started climbing the stairs again, glancing back at him. 'We're meeting upstairs, apparently. No idea what to expect, of course. But it's better than another night sat in front of the telly.'

Crystal followed her mother up the stairs. She should have stayed home in front of the telly. At least the television was not a challenge to her peace of mind. Not so long as she steered clear of the news channels, medical documentaries, and all shows set in hospitals, that was. The slightest thing could set her off these days, gloomily counting off the days, anticipating her own mortality.

Jack paused beside her. 'You okay?'

Typical of his sharp eyes to have spotted how easily tired she was.

'Fine,' she insisted stoutly, not yet ready to take him into her confidence.

She would probably never be ready, in fact. She hated the idea of people feeling sorry for her. Especially someone as fit and attractive as Jack.

'I like walking slowly, that's all. Unlike my mother. She loves stairs. I think she's part goat.'

Jack grinned with appreciation. 'Well, I have no relatives in the goat family, so I'll walk with you, if you don't mind,' he said, falling in beside her on the stairs. He glanced up at her mother's rapidly vanishing figure, now hurrying through the open door at the top. 'Quite an enthusiastic woman, your mother.'

'Tell me about it.'

She was laughing, but secretly Crystal was troubled. He could not have come tonight simply to see her again, could he? It was flattering. But she was not in the market for a relationship. Not even remotely.

She could have cried.

The times when she would have fallen on her knees and thanked her lucky stars for attracting the interest of someone nice like Jack. And here she was, throwing him back in the sea, for all the world like a bad fish.

The real irony was that Jack was too nice. Far too nice to be saddled with problems like hers. Serious, heartbreaking problems. She had to find a way of warning him off. But how, without sounding rude?

He took the last few stairs two at a time and opened the door at the top of the stairs, holding it for her. 'There you go.'

There was a corridor beyond, a door wedged open at the far end, with another COLOURING BOOK CLUB poster taped to the outside glass panel. Inside the room she could see her mum already in conversation with someone, and a long table set out with pens and paper and books, a few people already seated and colouring. There was a general buzz of chatter, and some soft music playing in the background.

She was probably going to hate every minute of this meeting.

'I'm not sure if I'll keep coming after tonight,' she told Jack, hesitating in front of the door.

'You don't know what it's like yet. It could be fun.'

'Now you sound like my mother.'

They were close together in the narrow corridor. Jack's smile was wry. He looked down into her eyes. 'Damn,' he said, 'that's not exactly how I planned to come across.'

Her heart began to thud.

Planned?

So he had come here to see her again. After only one brief conversation at the beach hut. Like he felt she was worth pursuing.

Little did he know.

'What do you do for a living?' he asked her suddenly.

Crystal was so taken aback that she answered honestly. 'Nothing, at the moment.' Then she shook her head. 'No, that's not entirely true. I help out at my mum's guesthouse.'

'Bed and breakfast? Turning down the sheets?' His eyebrows arched attractively, though she could see he was partly mocking her. 'I can't quite envisage you as a chambermaid.'

'Bit of a stretch?'

'To be honest, I had you down as more of a cerebral type. A high-powered business executive, maybe. With one of those revolving leather chairs and a team of lackeys.'

It was not so far from the kind of work she had done in London before she came home. But her early career success had been cut short by illness. Her damn body, betraying her just when she needed it most.

'I'm the only lackey these days,' she said huskily.

His gaze searched her face. 'No,' he said, suddenly serious, 'I don't see that at all. Quite impossible. You have that air about you.'

She looked back at him, curious now.

'What air?'

'That Queen-of-the-Universe air,' he said promptly. 'Like you were born to command armies.'

'Armies of lackeys?'

'Precisely.' He grinned, and then moved aside as someone else came hurrying up the library stairs. 'Sorry.'

It was a woman in a blue floral ankle-length dress. She looked a little older than Crystal, with generous hips and a lovely smile.

She paused and nodded to them both. 'Here for the colouring club?'

'That's right,' Crystal said before Jack could answer for her.

Closing his mouth, Jack glanced at her and raised his eyebrows again. She was not intimidated this time. That wry look must be a habitual expression of his.

'I'm Emma,' the woman introduced herself, shaking both their hands. Her grip was just right; neither too forceful nor too limp, and her interest in them felt genuine. 'Pleased to meet you both. I'm the organiser. I work here at the library, so if there's anything you need, just ask me.'

Jack introduced himself with a smile, adding, 'And this is Crystal.'

'We're not together,' Crystal said promptly.

The woman looked round at her in surprise, but made no comment. 'I think things are getting underway in there. Shall we?'

The first meeting of the colouring club started off in an undemanding fashion, Crystal thought, which was quite a relief. There were introductions round the table, with Emma noting down the names and smiling at each person, then she talked generally about how each meeting would operate.

'You can use any of the loose colouring sheets in the middle of the table, or borrow any of the club books. They've all been provided for your enjoyment, and the cost is included in the meeting charge.' She pointed to the old biscuit tin in the centre of the table, where most people had already deposited their money. 'Just be sure to sign your colourings, so we know whose artwork it is, and return the books to the pile at the end of each meeting.'

Emma smiled round at them all, then tucked a loose strand of dark hair behind one ear; the first sign of nervousness she had displayed since asking them all to sit down.

Crystal thought the club organiser looked like a very pleasant woman, if rather buttoned-up. In this part of Cornwall, so near the rugged north coast, people tended to take a more relaxed approach to life. In a place where sand got into everything, it was hard to insist on strict rules and regulations. But perhaps it was working in a library that did it.

All the same, Emma might have made a good friend, if Crystal had been in a position to make new friends.

Which she definitely wasn't, of course.

Everything in her life was on hold, at least for the time being. Maybe later, if …

'So, everyone should select a sheet or pattern book from the ones on the table, unless you brought your own books, and get colouring.' Emma consulted the large clock on the wall. 'We'll have tea and coffee with biscuits in about fifty minutes, also included in the meeting fee, but if anyone wants to bring cake to future meetings, that's fine too. We'll get another half an hour after the break to finish up our designs. At the end of the session, you can display your work to everyone else, if you like. But only if you feel comfortable doing so.'

Emma paused. 'The main thing is to have fun and make new friends, that's why we're all here. So please feel free to chat while colouring. Enjoy yourselves!'

She got up and put the music back on while everyone rummaged about on the table for a book. It was very restful, background music, all violins and pan-pipes, and it meant there was no awkward silence as everyone sorted out their pens and began to settle down and colour.

Clever, Crystal thought, and smiled at Emma.

In the chair opposite, her mum slid a selection of

books across the shiny table top. 'There you go, Crystal. I'm plumping for forest animals. What about you?'

'Oh, did you bring your own books?' Emma asked at once, leaning forward to admire their selection. 'How lovely. These look amazing.' She glanced at Crystal. 'Do you know which one you're going to choose?'

Shyly, Crystal held up her own current favourite book, page after page of beautiful seascapes with exotic fish, curling waves and leaping dolphins.

Emma looked at Jack, who made his wry face again. Her smile was sympathetic. 'Not sure yet?'

He sat back, letting her see the book of mandala designs he had brought. 'I'll probably crack on with one of these.'

'I love mandalas. So intricate to colour, yet restful at the same time. They really make you *think*.'

Jack grinned. 'Exactly.'

Watching them talk, Crystal was suddenly aware of a tiny stirring of jealousy. Which was ridiculous. Jack was not her property. She barely knew the guy. He had turned up here out of the blue, and there was nothing between them but air. Yet here she was, holding her breath as she listened to him chatting so easily with the club organiser. Quite as though he had come here with *her*, not on his own.

She must have been frowning, because Emma suddenly got up and walked round to the other side of the table, shooting her an apologetic smile on the way.

'What's everyone else colouring?' Emma asked lightly, and bent to look at Graham's book.

A middle-aged man with a thick moustache and a blue-striped polo-neck, Graham looked startled by this sudden incursion into his space. Nonetheless, he dutifully lowered his pen to let her see. 'Lions,' he muttered. 'With sunflowers in their mouths.'

Oh my god, Crystal thought, horribly embarrassed. She stared down at her dolphin design with sudden ferocious attention as though she had never seen it before. Now Emma thinks he's my boyfriend and that I'm annoyed with her for talking to him.

Bloody hell.

Jack glanced at her sideways. 'You okay?'

Why was everyone always asking her that, as though constantly assuming the opposite, that she was *not okay*?

Maybe her medication was making her prickly. But she felt abruptly angry and defensive.

She looked round at the others in the room. There was her and her mum Fiona, then Jack, the organiser Emma, Graham with his sunflower-munching lions, Penny and Helen – two thirty-something women in almost identical dresses who seemed to be besties and hadn't spoken to anyone else much – and Boris, a huge, gruff-voiced man in his late forties whose shaven head gleamed under the ceiling spotlights. He was probably the least likely colourist of them all, Crystal thought, and noticed her mum staring at his tattooed forearms. No doubt there would be some choice comments about Boris on the way home.

It was hard being seriously ill without much outward sign of it, and harder still to accept that she might need other people occasionally. When things went wrong, she had always muddled through on her own before the illness, and tried to be optimistic about the future. It had got her to a high-powered position in a top national company in a central London office

Now look at her, for goodness' sake. Reliant on her mum to ferry her back and forth for hospital visits, hanging out with this disparate crew, colouring in seascapes in an obscure Cornish library.

Not exactly the high life anymore, was it?

'Of course,' she told him, maybe a little too sharply. 'I'm perfectly fine. Why wouldn't I be?'

He continued to colour in his mandala without any sign of discomfort. 'My,' he said softly, 'what big teeth you have, Grandma.'

Across the table, her mum made a snorting sound that was suspiciously like laughter.

Bloody bloody bloody …

Crystal picked up a sharp lime green that was not even remotely colour-appropriate for a dolphin's snout, and began colouring in her picture with renewed passion, her brow furrowed with concentration. Thick bold strokes splashed carelessly over the computer-drawn lines, but she didn't care. At least, that's what she told herself, intent on her seascape.

Jack looked at what she was doing and raised his eyebrows again.

Oh no you don't, she thought fiercely.

Shifting in her seat, Crystal brought a protective arm round to shield her book from his gaze.

To her chagrin, he too laughed. 'Where do you live?' he asked suddenly, putting down his pen.

Crystal's lip curled. Straight to the point, huh? It was blindingly obvious that Jack had come here tonight just to see her, not to do any colouring. She was willing to be that he had never coloured in a picture in his life. Or not since he was at playschool, anyway.

'Nowhere,' she replied tightly.

'Homeless? I thought you said your mum had a bed and breakfast place?'

'Of course we do, ignore her.' Her mum instantly told him where they lived, apparently oblivious to Crystal's head shaking violently from side to side. 'You should come over sometime. I can always do with another pair of hands.'

'If only they sold spare pairs of hands,' Jack commented blithely, bending to examine his picture. 'In the supermarket. Three pairs for the price of two.'

'That would be so useful,' her mum agreed.

'So you wouldn't mind if I came over sometime. Do you have any odd jobs that need doing, then?'

'Always.' Her mum smirked at him. 'But come as a

friend, Jack. I wouldn't want you to think we only want you for your ... your *body*.'

'You mean my hands, don't you, Fiona?'

'Of course.' Her mum blushed. 'Such nice hands.'

'Seriously, I'm happy to do any jobs round the place if you're stuck.' He looked at Crystal pointedly. 'But I'd love to come over as a friend too. Maybe one evening next week. If you're sure I'd be welcome.'

'Oh, don't mind Crystal.' Her mum slipped her reading glasses down her nose a bit to admire her colouring from the correct distance. 'Mmm, that's not bad. Honestly, Crystal would love you to come round. She's only just landed from London and needs to make new friends here. Friends her own age. She's shy, that's all.'

Crystal sucked in her breath crossly. Shy?

Jack held Crystal's gaze for a long moment. Was that mockery in his face? 'Yes, I could tell immediately she was shy.'

'Mum ...' Crystal began threateningly.

'Yes, darling?'

She shut her mouth, seeing Jack's grin. 'Nothing.'

Selecting a thick black pen, she coloured in her lime-green dolphin's eye with more than necessary force. A big shiny black eye. Like the one she'd like to give her mum.

'So, Jack, do you have a girlfriend?' her mum asked, taking even Crystal off guard.

Jeez, talk about being transparent.

Hugely embarrassed and tempted to kick her mum under the table, Crystal raised her head and looked straight at Jack, surprising an odd expression on his face. Kind of defensive, and shuttered too, like he was hiding something from them. Clearly he had not liked her mum's question much either.

Now she was curious too, despite herself. It looked like her mum's question had not so much embarrassed Jack as caught him on the raw.

So did he have a girlfriend or not?

'Erm, no,' he said, after a short hesitation.

'You don't seem very sure about it,' her mum observed, a little sharply.

'I'm sure.'

'But you had a girlfriend? Recently?'

'Mum, for God's sake,' Crystal said.

'I'm only asking him one simple question,' her mum hissed back, and waved a lidless pink pen back and forth as though intending to throw it at her if she persisted. 'Nothing to get your knickers in a twist about.' She smiled brightly at Jack. 'So you did have a girlfriend, but now you don't.'

'That's right.'

'Hmm, I see.' Her mum slipped the lid back on the pink pen with a snap. Her sheer nosiness was out in the open now, her eyes avid as she leant over the table towards him. 'So what happened? You broke up with this girl?'

'No.'

'She broke up with you, then?'

'No.'

Her mum frowned. 'But you said –'

'She died.' Jack sat back in his chair, looking at them both, a dark red tinge along his cheekbones. 'Two years and three months ago, just before we were due to get married.'

CHAPTER FIVE

Goodness, this guy's got forearms like Popeye's, Emma thought, shaking Boris' large tattooed hand as he shuffled out of the meeting room, his shaven head bowed. He had the air of an old sea-dog too. Probably ate spinach regularly. Such an odd choice for a man like him, to come to a colouring book club at the local library. The last person she would have thought …

'Thank you for coming,' she called after him suddenly, feeling guilty at her thoughts. There was no set demographic for people who enjoyed colouring books and she hated any form of prejudice. 'Hope to see you again next time!'

He raised a hand in farewell as he went back down the stairs, but did not look back.

Emma frowned. She was sure she had seen Boris before.

But where?

Most of the other club members had left the meeting room now, many with a pleasing reluctance, needing to be reminded several times to put away their artwork. But a few were still buzzing around. Crystal and her mother, Fiona, for instance, who were still packing away their colouring books and pens, and chatting together. The young man called Jack was waiting for them to leave, an odd look on his face. *We're not together*, Crystal had made a point of saying when Emma introduced herself to the pair earlier, with what sounded like vehemence.

Yet the three of them did appear to be together, Jack even scrabbling under the table to rescue a lost felt tip for Fiona, who smiled down at him in a flustered way.

'I hope you'll all come again,' Emma told them cheerfully, pushing in chairs around the large meeting table.

'Absolutely,' Fiona assured her, and leant across to shake her hand. The older woman was looking a bit pink in the face, Emma thought. Perhaps it was all the excitement of colouring-in. Or maybe she was going through the menopause. Her own mum was forever complaining of sudden hot flushes and odd moods. 'It was so lovely to meet you, and the others too. I really enjoyed myself. In fact, we all enjoyed ourselves.'

'Excellent.'

'And I'm sure we'll be here for the next meeting.' Fiona glanced at her daughter, who was looking rather pale by contrast with her mother. 'Isn't that right, Crystal?'

Crystal said something that Emma did not catch, and hurried out of the room as though desperate to leave.

'Sorry.' Her mother shrugged and then disappeared after her daughter with pursed lips, as though she disapproved of her abrupt behaviour.

Surprised and a little concerned, Emma watched the two women leave. Had it been something she said? She could not help wondering if Crystal and Jack were having a lovers' tiff, despite the younger woman's initial insistence that they were not together. But maybe Crystal was late for something, or wasn't feeling quite right. Her face had been quite pale, after all.

Maybe Crystal was pregnant too, and feeling under the weather. She could certainly identify with that, Emma thought wryly.

Jack nodded at her pleasantly enough though, hands in his jeans pockets, and whistled on his way down the stairs. She had seen the grim look in his face though, seconds before his defences crashed down to cover it, and knew the careless whistling was an act. The young man was upset and desperate to hide it from her.

Oh, she certainly knew all about *that*.

Emma began clearing away the remnants of the meeting. She needed to keep busy and not let her mind wander back to her situation. But just as she was finishing up, her phone buzzed in her bag.

She dug it out, frowning at the screen.

It was a text from her mum.

Still on for that coffee tomorrow? I'll be in town, shopping. Where do you want to meet up? Not the house, we've got decorators in.

Tomorrow was her day off. As good a time as any to make her confession, she had thought, leaving a message on her mum's answerphone earlier. But she had hoped to have their chat at home, not in public. Still, it was better to get it over with.

She texted back a terse, *Yes.* Then hesitated, unsure where to suggest that would be public but not so quiet their conversation might be overheard.

A sudden thought struck her.

How about the beach café, 11am?

Thirty seconds later, her phone buzzed again.

See you there. Assuming I can drag your father away from his allotment, that is. We can't wait to hear this 'exciting news' of yours!

Emma groaned, and threw her phone back into the depths of her handbag. She had decided that she needed to tell her parents about the baby as soon as possible, as it could have a bearing on her final decision. She was not looking forward to the actual moment of 'fessing up. It would be embarrassing and humiliating. 'I had sex with a total stranger in Ibiza and now I'm carrying his child.'

Hers had never been the kind of parents who

welcomed such intimate confessions. But she badly needed to know what her mum and dad thought first. After all, with their support, maybe she could embrace life as a single mum instead.

The very thought of facing pregnancy and motherhood alone, never even able to contact the father of her child, brought her to tears.

'Oh, not again,' she said to herself sternly, and patted her eyes with a tissue. She had done enough blubbing these past few days. It was time to grow up. 'This baby is your own fault, Emma. Crying isn't going to do you any good.'

Before closing the book, Emma glanced down at the picture she had been colouring in during the meeting. It was a gorgeous medieval waterscape, complete with a Lady of Shalott lookalike drifting down a river in a high-prowed boat, surrounded by weeping willows and yellow flag irises. The blues and greens and yellows of the artwork were peaceful and clean, and a thousand years away from the mad bustle of her everyday life. It had felt lovely to forget her troubles for an hour while colouring it in. But a few moments of tearful reflection had brought her back to the cold truth of reality.

This was a dilemma she could not sidestep with a few hours' quiet colouring. But maybe family would provide the answer. Maybe tomorrow's meet-up with her mum and dad would reinforce her painful decision not to continue with the pregnancy.

She couldn't have this baby. It was impossible.

'Oh, Crystal. Good to see you're up at last.'

Perched on a breakfast stool, Crystal looked up from her bowl of soggy cereal. She had been unable to sleep all night and had finally given up the attempt at about five o'clock in the morning, sitting up to read a book instead. But she bit back her ready retort, forcing a smile instead. Her mum would not understand and might even fear it indicated some worsening of her condition.

The last thing she wanted right now was to be nagged about early nights and proper sleeping patterns, like she was still a teenager.

'Did you need me, Mum?'

'Well, as a matter of fact …' Her mum was lurking in the doorway to the kitchen. 'The guests have all had their breakfasts and gone out for the day, but I'm expecting some new arrivals after lunch. Could you mind the place for a couple of hours?'

Crystal pushed away her cereal. She was not very hungry anyway. 'Of course.'

'And maybe run the hoover over the carpet in Number Three again? I can't get rid of the sand those surfers left behind. One of the hazards of renting out rooms so near the beach.' Her mum tutted, zipping up a large sports hold-all and swinging it over her shoulder. 'Surfers! Nasty mucky pups, some of them. But we need the custom.'

Suspicious, Crystal frowned at the hold-all. 'What have you got in there?'

'Nothing.'

'Looks a bit on the heavy side for a bag containing nothing.'

Her mum made a face. 'All right, no need to make a fuss. It's a …' She coughed, masking the words.

'A what?'

'Wit shoe,' her mother managed, coughing violently again.

'A wit shoe?'

'Shoot, shoot.'

'A wit shoot?'

Cough. Cough. Cough. 'Yes, a …' Cough. 'Wit shoot.'

'Mum, what on earth are you talking about? And stop coughing, you'll give yourself a sore throat.'

'Maybe I'm coughing *because* I've got a sore throat,' her mother retorted.

'Nonsense, there's nothing wrong with you that a sharp

pinch wouldn't sort out.' Crystal narrowed her eyes on her mum's flushed face. 'Come on, out with it. Where are you going with this "wit shoot"?'

'Oh, just … down there.' Her mum shrugged, gesticulating vaguely over her shoulder. 'You know.'

'Down where?'

'To the … um … beach.'

'The beach?' Crystal stared. Then her mouth gaped. '*Wit shoot*. Oh my god. You weren't trying to say *wet suit*, were you?'

Her mother glared at the clock on the kitchen wall. 'Goodness, is that the time? Really, I'd better hurry or I'll be late.'

'Mum, are you going *surfing*?'

'No.' Her mother sounded outraged. She paused, thought for a moment, then corrected herself. 'Yes.'

'I'm sorry?'

'All right, you've got me. Truth be told, I've been very silly and agreed to have a surfing lesson. I'm sure I won't actually go surfing on my first lesson though. But I bought a wet suit just in case. Because … well, the sea's very cold, isn't it?'

'It certainly is.'

Her mum turned to go. 'So I'll just be off, then. You mind the B and B, and I'll have my surfing lesson.'

'Hang on, not so fast. Why are you suddenly having lessons in surfing? And who's giving you this lesson?'

'Nobody.'

Crystal raised her eyebrows.

Her mum grimaced at her expression of disbelief. 'Oh, bloody hell. All right, it's a man. A man I've met.'

'You met a man?'

'The other night. At the colouring book club.'

Crystal was staggered. 'I didn't see you talking to any men. Except Jack.' Her eyes widened in horror. 'It's not Jack, is it?'

'Of course not. I'm not a cradle snatcher. Besides,

Jack's only got eyes for you.'

'Well, that's his problem. Because I'm not in the market for … Well, for anything really.' She realised that she was being gently derailed. 'So what man was this?'

Her mum sucked in her breath, then said abruptly, 'He was that man with the shaven head.'

Crystal's mouth couldn't get much wider. 'The man with the shaven head? The one with … *tattoos*?'

'He may have had the odd tattoo, yes. I really didn't pay that much attention. He was a very nice man. We had a lovely chat about …'

'About?' Crystal prompted her.

'Biscuits.'

'You talked about biscuits?'

'Why not? He's very interested in biscuits, as it happens.' Her mother sniffed. 'As am I.'

Crystal remembered the man clearly. Shaven head, tattoos, darkly tanned skin, huge bulging forearms like a sailor.

'Are you kidding me?'

'For goodness' sake, why would I joke about something like that? We both agreed the biscuits at the refreshments break were pretty poor, that's all. Supermarket brand variety pack, did you have any? Horrid limp little things. Anyway, he said he liked a nice crisp Garibaldi. I told him I prefer chocolate digestives, those thick ones with ribbing.' She smiled girlishly. 'He had such a nice smile.'

Crystal felt like she was going mad. 'And now you're going surfing with him?'

'Having a lesson. He teaches surfing. And runs the beach café. That nice one on the front, right below the beach huts.'

'Why didn't I see you talking to this guy?'

'You were in the loo.'

'Mum, listen –'

'No, my mind's made up. And I'm late now, thanks to you. I'm having a surfing lesson from Boris this morning, then we're going to dry off and enjoy a nice cup of coffee together in his café.' She marched towards the front door, the large holdall bouncing on her shoulder. 'And you're not going to stop me.'

Still quite shocked, Crystal listened to the front door slam resoundingly behind her mother. 'I wouldn't dream of trying,' she said, then got up to clear the breakfast counter.

He had such a nice smile.

She frowned, putting her bowl in the dishwasher.

Was her mother seriously looking for love? Or was this just some momentary madness that would pass after a few surfing lessons? She wanted her mum to be happy, of course. It wasn't the fact that Fiona was dating again that was a problem. It was her mother's odd taste in men.

'Why can it never be an accountant? Or a bank manager?' Crystal shook her head. 'Just someone *normal* would do.'

Heading upstairs a moment later, she felt a nasty twinge inside. Then she doubled over in pain, groaning loudly.

Thank goodness all the guests had gone out for the day.

'God, that hurts.' Stumbling into their private bathroom at the far end of the landing, Crystal stared at herself in the mirror above the sink. She looked very pale, her eyes red-rimmed, her lips a little blue. 'Damn it.'

Was it the shock of her middle-aged mother dating a Popeye lookalike that had caused this, or was she launching into another full-blown 'episode'?

Opening the bathroom cabinet, she studied the array of medication, then took two mild painkillers with some water. The doctors had told her she could not take anything too strong, or it could cause internal bleeding – or worse.

'I'm not going back into hospital,' she promised herself in the mirror, gripping hard onto the cold rim of the sink. 'Not again.'

She stood there a few minutes, until the nausea had

subsided. The blueness started to ebb away from her lips, and she was able to breathe more easily.

Perhaps she ought to lie down though. Just in case.

Then the doorbell rang.

Emma meandered slowly down the road to the beach, taking her time, enjoying the sunshine. She was not in any hurry to make her fateful announcement to her parents. The Atlantic was ruffled, a glorious deep blue capped with white rollers as the tide rolled inexorably up the sand. There were surfers in the water today. Emma could see parents and tots standing about in the shallows too, and some intrepid canoeists further out, shouting to each other as they paddled furiously back and forth across the bay.

The beach café was busy, as the tourist season was starting to get underway, but not so busy that she couldn't find a table.

Her mum and dad were not there yet, so she went to the counter to order herself a coffee.

The man who turned to serve her had a shaven head and tattoos everywhere. He stared, then gave her an awkward grin, showing several front teeth missing.

'Hello again,' he said gruffly.

It was Boris, one of the men from the colouring club. The one who had reminded her of Popeye.

Emma smiled at him warmly. 'I knew I'd seen you somewhere before.' She glanced about the beach café. 'This is your place, isn't it?'

'Been here nearly two years now. I teach surfing too, during the peak season. Bought this place when I retired from the …' Boris hesitated, and she saw an odd look in his face. 'Navy,' he finished, but she felt sure he was lying.

'But how marvellous.'

Boris wiped down the counter, looking embarrassed. 'Well, that's enough about me. What can I get you?'

'A large latte, please. But with only one shot of espresso.' She smiled apologetically. 'I can't handle strong coffee.'

'Coming right up.'

Emma watched as Boris turned away to make the latte. She grinned with sudden understanding. It had not been a mere whim last night when she told her parents to meet her at the beach café. Her unconscious must have been nagging at her, telling her precisely where she had seen Boris before. Here, at the small café right on the seafront.

Some more customers wandered in, making for the ice cream counter, and Boris shouted through a hatch into the kitchen, 'Matthew? You're needed.'

The door swung open. A man appeared in the doorway, taller than Boris, broad-shouldered and fair-haired, and stood there, wiping his hands on his white chef's half-apron.

'What was that you said, Dad?' he asked, his tone clipped as though annoyed at having been disturbed.

He looked straight across at Emma as he spoke, his blue eyes intent on her face, and she felt her heart miss a beat.

Only hearts don't really do that, she told herself bluntly. Probably just indigestion. She had wolfed down her breakfast yoghurt rather quickly this morning.

'Folk needing ice cream,' Boris muttered, inclining his head towards the mother and child waiting patiently to be served. 'You're not cooking. Go on, you can dole out a few Whippies.'

But Matthew did not move, his gaze on Emma's face.

Boris looked round at him irritably, then saw who he was looking at. He straightened, leaving her latte unmade. 'Oh, this is Emma, from the colouring book club last night. She's the organiser, the lady I was telling you about.' He hesitated. 'Emma, this is my son, Matthew.'

Emma forced herself to sound calm. Despite the fact that her heart was now performing somersaults in her chest.

'Hello.' She sounded about twelve and breathy.

Matthew nodded, saying nothing. But his eyes never left her face.

Emma reckoned he must be about her age, maybe even early thirties. Drop dead gorgeous too. In fact, Matthew was so good-looking that she actually found herself staring at him too, and then had to look away, horribly embarrassed.

'Hello, darling.'

Her mother's voice behind him gave Emma the perfect excuse to turn away. 'Hi, Mum,' she said, flustered.

Her father was there too, his forehead red from the sun despite his cap. No doubt he had been gardening in his allotment all morning and forgot to put the cap on without her mum there to nag at him.

'Hello, Dad.'

Her parents both kissed Emma on the cheek, then spent a few pointless minutes squabbling over what everyone wanted to eat and drink. Not an easy decision, as whatever her father wanted, her mother insisted on vetoing. All the while, she was aware of Matthew watching her, though he had moved away to serve the people waiting for ice cream at the other counter.

'Oh,' her dad said suddenly, staring at the wall menu, 'look at that. They do all-day breakfasts here. With black pudding too. I've not had an all-day breakfast with black pudding in years.'

'Bad for your heart, darling,' her mum said sharply. 'Have a nice black coffee instead. You'll thank me for it.'

'I doubt that,' her dad muttered.

'You haven't forgotten what the doctor said, have you? Besides, black coffee is very good for you. Strengthens the sinews.'

'I don't give a tuppenny bit about my sinews.' Her father nodded across the counter at Boris, who had been following this exchange with barely disguised disbelief. 'I'd like a Cornish cream tea, please.'

'Sorry, absolutely not.' Her mother countermanded the

order, then turned to glare at her husband. 'A cream tea? Are you insane? All-butter scones? Strawberry jam? Cornish clotted cream? You might as well sign your own death warrant.' Her mum smiled officiously at Boris, lowering her voice. 'He'll have an Americano, no milk. And I'd like a cappuccino. With a flapjack. Thanks ever so much.'

Boris repeated drily, 'Coming right up.'

Matthew had finished serving the mum and toddler their ice creams, who were now leaving with satisfied smiles and two deep-filled and sprinkled cornets. He strolled back over as though to help his dad with the order.

'Nothing to eat for you, then?' he asked Emma, studying her closely with a look that made her insides go all wobbly.

'No, thanks.'

'I can't tempt you with a flapjack?'

She swallowed, her gaze locked to his, not even glancing at the array of inviting goodies laid out on the counter.

'I'm not hungry,' she lied.

Matthew nodded, still watching her. 'I don't think I've ever seen you in here before.'

'I've been in a few times.'

'Before I started helping out here, I expect. I would have remembered you.'

'So you don't usually work here?'

His face tightened. 'I worked in an office before. My father-in-law's office.'

Oh crap, he's married, she thought, and her stomach plummeted horribly.

'But then I sued for divorce, and it was … a bit awkward. So my dad offered me work here instead.'

Emma tried not to beam at him in relief.

Not married. Or at least was in the process of getting unmarried.

'I can see how that would have been awkward.'

He nodded. 'Especially since we'd never particularly got on.'

'With your wife?'

'With my father-in-law. I was too much of an outdoors type for him. He and Chelsea are more into watching telly.'

'Chelsea?'

'My wife.' He paused, looking away. 'Ex-wife, soon.' There was an odd note in his voice. Sadness? Regret?

'Right,' she agreed weakly, trying her hardest not to stare at his broad shoulders and powerful chest.

She wondered if, despite his comments, he was still a little bit in love with his ex.

Her mum bumped her arm, apparently oblivious to the metaphorical drool on her daughter's chin. 'Emma, we're going to sit outside. It's too sunny to be indoors on a day like this. You coming?'

'I need to pay.'

'Okeydokey. But let me know what we owe you. Our treat, yes?' She glanced from Emma's face to Matthew's as though suddenly aware of some tension in the air. 'You sure you can manage, love?'

Emma murmured something that might have been, 'Yes, of course,' and her mum disappeared outside with her dad. She fumbled ridiculously with her purse while Matthew rang up the sale on the till. Somehow she managed to hand him the correct money without dropping her bag to the floor when their hands touched, too briefly.

'Oh,' she said, pulling back her hand.

His smile was knowing. Damn him. He must have noticed her staring. Hopefully he had not spotted her salivating too.

'Anything else I can help you with?'

She shook her head wordlessly.

'Don't worry about the rest of the order. My dad's giving a surfing lesson in a few minutes, so I'll be taking over out here. I'll put it all on a tray and carry it out for you.'

'Thanks.'

'Emma, isn't it?' he checked.

She nodded.

'Matthew. Good to meet you, Emma.'

He held out his hand, and she took it as though in a dream. His handshake was firm and cool, and somehow perfect. She held the pose rather too long, so that her cheeks grew hot and she had to look away before this man saw how unspeakably sexy and attractive she found him.

Matthew was not finished with her though. 'So you run a colouring book club?'

'Just starting to, yes.'

'Should I come along next time? Keep my dad company? What do you think?'

Matthew wanted to come along to the colouring book club? This man wanted to sit opposite her, and colour in some masterpiece while she watched his bold pen stroking back and forth, and imagined …

Her tongue felt thick and rubbery. Somehow actual words had become impossible. Yet some kind of response was clearly required or she might never see this man again. Which would be a tragedy of epic proportions.

Emma nodded mutely, made a few humming noises under her breath, then picked up her latte and smiled at him. Next thing she knew, she was outside in the sunshine, too dazzled to see where she was going.

'Over here, love,' her mum called, waving at her from a rectangular wooden table with a large pink and white umbrella in the centre, providing some welcome shade.

Oh my God, Emma was thinking blindly. Oh my flipping God.

Matthew.

So there was such a thing as insta-lust. And it was not very comfortable to experience.

'Where's my flapjack?' her mother asked.

'Coming,' Emma told her, and collapsed on the bench seat in the shade. Her mouth was dry and she felt flushed and off-balance. Though perhaps that was the pregnancy, not the guy she had just been mentally panting over. 'Coming any minute.'

Her dad took off his cap and she noticed that his bald spot had grown larger, poor thing. But his smile was warm and encouraging. 'We've missed you round the house, love. How's life at the flat treating you?'

Emma sat up. Guilt stirred inside her, and abruptly the handsome man in the café was forgotten. There was no point dreaming about him anyway, not in her condition.

Her dad looked at her very oddly. Had he guessed what this was about? But no, how on earth could anyone guess?

She was not showing yet, would not be showing for another month or two at least. And outside work she always preferred to wear floor-sweeping, loose dresses and big comfortable over-shirts, nothing too clinging or revealing. No, her parents could not possibly have guessed. And since they both knew perfectly well that she did not have a boyfriend, it was unlikely they ever would if she was not about to confess to her idiocy, her carelessness.

'Actually, that's one reason I asked you here for a chat,' she began, then could not finish, suddenly unsure how to explain what had happened.

She must have rehearsed this speech a few dozen times, determined to get it right. Yet now she was here, with both her parents looking back at her in mild surprise, and the sound of the sea in her ears, all those carefully-prepared words failed her.

Her mother's eyes widened in alarm. 'You don't want to move back in with us, do you? It's too late for that. The decorators are there now. They're converting your old bedroom into a home gym for your father.' She patted her husband's hand. 'So he can look after his heart.'

Her dad made a face, but said nothing.

Emma looked from her mother to her father, then back again. A thought struck her. 'Well, say I did want to move back in at some point, would that be possible?'

'But you said you wanted your independence,' her mum pointed out, reasonably enough, though her voice was rising. 'It was your choice to move out, remember? You said you couldn't stand living with us. You said you needed a place of your own.'

'I remember.' She couldn't deny any of that. 'I know what I said, and I'm sorry.'

Her mum did not look very sympathetic. 'So what's changed?'

'Now hang on a minute, Sheila. No need to jump down the poor girl's throat.' Her dad took her hand across the table and squeezed it. His voice deepened. 'You all right, love? You look a bit peaky.'

Emma did not know what to say.

'You're not sickening for something, are you?' Her mother looked even more horrified. 'I can't have germs around your father. Not with his chest the way it is.'

'Mum, Dad,' Emma said abruptly, 'I'm pregnant.'

In the shocked silence that followed this announcement, a shadow fell over the patio beside her.

Emma, feeling a little hot and dizzy, glanced down at the broad-shouldered shadow, then up at Matthew.

His sharp blue eyes intent on her face, he was standing next to their table, a tray in his hands. It was obvious from his expression that he'd heard her blunt admission of impending motherhood. But Matthew did not react, merely holding out the tray towards them.

'Two coffees and a flapjack?'

CHAPTER SIX

Crystal threw open the door just as the bell rang again, insistently. It was Jack on the doorstep, leaning against the porch wall. He straightened when she opened the door, and looked her up and down.

'You look awful. Have I come at a bad time?'

Crystal could not believe his persistence. Or his lack of chivalry.

'I'm busy,' she said. 'My mum's just popped out and I'm minding the fort. What are you doing here?'

He was unabashed by her blunt approach. 'Your mum invited me to come round. So I've come round.'

Bemused, Crystal stared at her unwelcome visitor, wondering what on earth his problem could be.

It was clear what *her* problem was, on the other hand.

Him.

'To be honest,' she pointed out sweetly, 'it was more likely a figure of speech than a straight invitation.'

His smile annoyed her. 'To be honest, I don't care. I've never been one for metaphors.'

He said nothing more. The way he was looking at her was disturbing though. It was hard not to be aware of him. Sexually aware. And that kind of distraction, she could do without right now and did not enjoy. Not even remotely.

'So what do you want?'

'For us to talk.' Jack paused, still smiling. His eyes were a kind of dark velvety brown. Spine-tinglingly attractive, like the rest of him. Too bloody attractive, she thought crossly, scowling back at him. 'There are a few things I'd like to say to you.'

'Such as?'

'Let me in and I'll tell you.'

'I'm flattered,' she told him. 'But I'm too busy for a chat, sorry. Maybe another time.'

Jack stuck his foot in the door as she tried to close it, his palm flat on the door panel. 'Hang on, I haven't finished.'

'Well, I have.'

'Crystal, please …'

The anguish in his voice made Crystal pause and look at him properly, unable to ignore the tug of an answering anguish in her own heart.

His girlfriend had died a couple of years ago; he had told them that bare fact at the colouring book club. Not a sob story, intended to gain him sympathy. She had seen genuine pain in his eyes, a memory he could not erase. He had not elaborated at the time, not told them the circumstances of his girlfriend's death. But she could see he wanted to, especially now her mother was not here to complicate matters. And part of her wanted to hear him out. To know exactly what had happened to put that agony in his eyes.

Was her constant physical pain affecting her judgement? Was she being too hard on this guy?

Crystal sighed, then stepped back, letting the door open wider. 'You'd better come in. It's obvious I'm not going to get rid of you until you've had your say.'

'Thank you.'

'I just hope I'm not going to regret this.'

Crystal led Jack into the public lounge of her mother's guesthouse. It was the largest and most comfortable room in the house, and glorious sunshine was streaming in across the bare wooden floor. She had always loved its homely feel, her mum's taste in décor very evident in this room, with a wicker basket of logs artfully arranged on the hearth waiting for autumn days and a series of deep blue acrylic seascapes hanging above the mantel.

Jack looked about the room, and she saw that look on his face again. A look of anguish being held back by an iron will.

It was a look she was more accustomed to find on her own face in the mirror each morning.

'Please, sit down,' she told him.

Her instincts were screaming at her not to drag this chat out any further, that it could be dangerous. After all, nothing useful or good could possibly come from them developing any kind of friendship with each other. Crystal knew that for sure, even if he didn't.

Yet she was still curious to know what he had to say.

Jack seated himself on the blue sofa. But she could tell from the awkward way he crossed one leg over the other, then instantly changed position again, that he was uncomfortable even about sitting down. There was a constant restlessness about him; it made her wonder if he preferred to stand whenever possible.

Crystal had made tea, aware that this could be a longer conversation than she had intended. She handed him a mug of tea.

Jack accepted his drink with barely a glance. 'Thanks.'

'*De nada.*'

'My girlfriend's name was Beverley,' he told her. 'We'd been going out together since university. That's where we met.'

'You don't need to tell me about her if you don't want to,' she said, half hoping he would get up and leave.

'I do want to.'

So much for that, she thought gloomily.

Crystal sat opposite him in the armchair, even though there was plenty of room beside him on the sofa.

'We were madly in love,' he continued, staring at the seascapes over the fireplace as though looking out of a window. 'People always say that, don't they? But in our case it was true. It was like we were made for each other. Soul mates.'

Inexplicably, she felt jealous. Not of the unfortunate girlfriend who had died, but that he had met someone he could love so deeply. She had been in love, of course. But it had not lasted. She had never met someone with whom she had ever clicked in that breath-stealing way other people had described to her, or that she had seen in books and movies. It had always been a bit hit-and-miss, more her settling for someone she did not positively dislike than someone who made her heart beat harder.

Sometimes she wondered if, deep-down, there was something actually wrong with her. Something missing that everyone else could access at will. A sort of love hormone that overpowered logic and common sense, and made life somehow brighter, more exciting.

Perhaps struck by her silence, Jack glanced across at her, one eyebrow raised. 'Do you know what I mean?'

'Absolutely.'

'We knew from the start that we wanted to get married and start a family. Beverley worked in admin after university, so she took care of all the arrangements. She loved every minute of the process, even when things went wrong, as they sometimes did. She just got straight on with it. Always worked the problem, found a solution. She spent every spare moment sorting out her bridesmaids, getting all the dresses measured and made, designing a wedding cake, booking our honeymoon trip.' He smiled, as though amused by the memory of all that frenetic activity. Yet it was a sad, faraway smile too. 'Beverley wouldn't even let my mum get involved. That was how determined she was for our big day to be perfect, for everything to go exactly as planned.'

He paused, and Crystal looked away. There was a lump in her throat.

'Beverley was a keep-fit fanatic, used to go running every other day after work. Belonged to a local club, ran a few half-marathons.' He sipped his tea, his long lashes masking the expression in his eyes. 'Then she decided she wanted to run a marathon. Her first big race.'

It was so warm and sunny in the lounge, Crystal felt almost suffocated. Outside the windows, a breeze off the sea was stirring green swathes of large-leaved clematis growing up the garden wall. A bee knocked its heavy body against the window a few times, buzzing drowsily in the sunshine, then flew away.

'It was to raise money for the local hospice, Beverley's favourite charity. Her grandma had died there the year before, so …'

He swallowed hard.

Crystal sat forward, gazing at him sympathetically.

'She decided to run in her wedding dress, even though my mum told her it was unlucky for people to see it before the big day. But Beverley wouldn't listen. She thought she'd get more sponsorship for the hospice that way, and that was the only thing she cared about.'

He put down his mug of tea on a side table, unfinished. 'It was a hot day, really high temperatures. Beverley was about three miles from the finish line when she collapsed.'

'Oh God.'

'A heart attack. The doctor said it was probably brought on by the heat. They got her straight into an ambulance, but she died on her way to hospital.' Jack looked at her sombrely. 'I never even got a chance to say goodbye.'

'I'm so sorry.'

He nodded, not looking at her. 'That was over two years ago now. The first year was the worst. I expected that. But the second year …' He shook his head. 'I started having nightmares. I felt it was my fault, that I ought to have put my foot down, stopped her running that marathon. She might have listened to me.'

'It doesn't sound like it,' Crystal said, maybe a little too sharply.

To her relief, Jack was not offended though. 'No, you're probably right. Beverley never took advice from anyone. She knew what she wanted and always went all out to get it.'

'It wasn't your fault she died.'

'I know.'

She stood up and went to the window, and opened it a crack. The cool air was a relief. Her pain had come back. It felt like someone had punched her in the stomach. But she said nothing.

'I wanted to tell you about Beverley because I didn't want it hanging over us.' His voice had become brooding. 'I've met women before, women I've liked. And not told them about Beverley until … Well, until after we've had a few dates. That approach has never been much of a success, so I thought I'd get my history out the way first. Before even asking you.'

'Asking me?' she echoed, and looked back at him, suddenly confused. 'Asking what?'

'If you'll have dinner with me.'

She found herself just staring at him, stunned into silence. She ought to have seen this coming, she realised, and made it more obvious that she wasn't interested.

Except she *was* interested.

Jack got up and stood there, studying her face with a quick frown. 'You look surprised.'

'That's because I am.'

'Look, it's only dinner. Not a major commitment. What do you like to eat? Indian food? Chinese?' Jack paused, still watching her. She could see he was genuinely trying to puzzle her out. 'Or would you prefer something more casual, like a pub meal?'

She shook herself, coming back to reality with a cold sensation down her spine. For a moment there, she had looked into his eyes and been tempted by the idea …

'I'm sorry, I can't.'

'Can't have dinner with me?' He tilted his head to one side, as though thinking hard. His tone was level. 'Why not? Is there someone else?'

She was not going to lie.

'No,' she admitted.

'So why not come out with me? Unless …' Jack raised his eyebrows. 'Do you prefer women? Is that it?'

Her eyes widened. 'No, no, I just …' She did not know where to look. 'Look, sorry, I can't date anyone right now.'

'Too busy with work? I can understand that.' His smile nearly undid her resolve. 'Don't think of it as a date, then. Come out for dinner with me as a friend.'

If only she could. But it would be so dangerous to say yes. The chemistry between them was undeniable.

It would be unfair on him too.

The pain in her stomach felt like an ulcer eating away at her. Which was probably exactly what it was. Internal bleeding. Her body was falling apart. The only thing holding her together these days was the medication. And that would not work forever; the doctors had been very clear on that point.

Slowly, she released the breath she had been holding for what felt like ages. 'Jack, I can't. I'm really sorry.'

She saw a flash of hurt in his eyes, then he was smiling again. 'Okay, fair enough. I'm sorry for pressing you so hard.'

But he was still hoping she would change her mind, she could hear it in his voice. The silence in the room hurt so badly, twisting her inside-out with sheer frustration, she wanted to scream. But she resisted the urge, keeping all that pointless emotion out of her face. It was only a date. But even one dinner date could raise her hopes beyond what was reasonable and fair to both of them.

Jack was kind, and sexy with it. He deserved better than her. He deserved someone whole. Someone with a future.

'You're not my type, that's all,' she said.

Liar, her heart screamed. *Liar, liar.*

But what else could she do? How else could she put him off without admitting the truth? And she was not ready for people to know yet. Certainly not for this man to know. He would pity her. And that would be too humiliating to bear.

'Right.' He glanced down at his cold tea, then at the door. 'I'll let myself out.'

She remained standing until he had gone, then fell to her knees on the wooden floor. The pain writhed inside her like a red-hot worm.

Damn it to hell.

Crystal did not know how long she stayed on the floor of the lounge, staring at nothing, trying to cope with the pain in her stomach until it finally ebbed away. But she could not stay there forever. Someone might ring the doorbell again or call on the telephone, and she would need to answer, to sound normal. Or her mother might come home again and be worried. She did not want to worry anyone.

She forced herself back to her feet and stumbled upstairs. Her bedroom was at the back of the guesthouse. It felt small and chilly after the generous warmth of the lounge. Nonetheless, it was sanctuary of a kind. She lay on the narrow bed for a while, thinking over what she had said and done. Remembering the hurt look in Jack's face.

Eventually she rolled over on the bed and dragged open her top bedside drawer.

Inside were some documents, and a few glossy pamphlets. She scooped them out and spread them across her bed, studying each title in turn.

What To Expect When The Call Comes
Pre-Transplant Patient Education Handbook

Living with a Life-Limiting Condition

Struck by sudden dizziness, Crystal gave a groan. The words danced in front of her eyes.

'Bloody hell.'

What she really wanted was to tip all these gloomy hospital pamphlets back into the drawer, change into her shorts and walk over to the beach hut for a few lazy hours. It was such a beautiful day. But she had promised her mum she'd stay at the guesthouse in case tonight's new arrivals tried to check in early, and she didn't want to break her promise.

Crystal picked up the *Pre-Transplant Patient Education Handbook* and flicked through it for about the tenth time. She always hated what she learnt in its coolly impersonal and briskly-worded pages, but it was important to understand what might lie ahead.

'Come on, woman,' she said sternly, sitting up with a straight back. 'Feeling sorry for yourself is not going to change anything.'

She settled on the section grimly entitled, "The Final Stages of Liver Failure," and began to read.

CHAPTER SEVEN

'Emma, this gentleman would like to speak to you,' Harold said, appearing at her counter in the Reference area. 'Do you have a moment?'

Gentleman?

Emma looked up from the computer monitor, smiling automatically, and felt the air rush out of her lungs.

She had expected some elderly, bespectacled man, maybe with a grey felt hat or tweed coat. Someone unassuming and inoffensive. That was the image her brain had conjured when she heard the word, 'gentleman'.

Instead she got the absolute opposite.

This 'gentleman' was not much older than thirty, athletic-looking, broad-shouldered, fair-haired, and with piercing blue eyes that met hers with every indication of irony.

It was Matthew, the guy from the beach café. The one who had overheard her embarrassing announcement.

'I'm pregnant,' she had told them abruptly, and the silence had been electric. Then this joker, thick blond fringe flopping in his eyes, had held out his serving tray and offered them a flapjack.

She said nothing, but her right hand clenched into a

fist.

A magical moment indeed.

Matthew gave her a tentative smile. 'Hi again, remember me?'

How could I forget?

'Thanks,' she told Harold, her smile still frozen in place. She did not want her colleague to suspect what was going on. Not that anything was going on, of course. But she did not want Harold to suspect anything. At all. 'You can leave it with me. I'll deal with this … gentleman.'

With a cheery nod, Harold bustled away again.

She looked at Matthew, at her most icily polite. 'Can I help you?'

'I just wanted a quick word.'

'Fire ahead.'

'Is there somewhere quieter we can talk?'

Quizzically, she looked around the building. Nearby, a few absorbed readers were browsing the shelves, others sitting silently at desks with their heads bent over reference tomes or clicking through websites on the free-to-use computers provided. It wasn't a mum-and-toddler morning, so even the kids' section on the other side of the building was relatively quiet today.

'We're in a library.'

'Right, yeah, sorry.' He held out a hand. 'I'm Matthew, from the –'

'I remember who you are.'

'Right.' He nodded slowly, meeting her gaze again. 'The flapjack thing. Sorry about that. Bad timing.'

'You think?'

His look was apologetic. 'Look, I don't have long. I had some errands to run in town for my dad. He said you worked here.'

'As you see.'

'I only popped in on my way back to work because …' He grimaced, appearing to struggle with himself. 'I just wanted to ask, is it okay if I come to the colouring book club too?'

'Of course. Everyone's welcome at the club.'

Though she could not believe he was suddenly interested in colouring. He looked more like the type who plays rugby at the weekends, then drinks himself into oblivion at the pub afterwards. Not takes up colouring in pictures for pleasure.

'Great.' He voiced her thought with spooky accuracy. 'Not that I'm hugely into colouring.'

She raised her eyebrows. 'But you want to try it out?'

'Not really.'

'I'm sorry, you just said –'

'I want to keep an eye on my dad. My dad and this other woman, to be frank.'

'Boris?'

He nodded. 'He met her at your colouring club, you see. And ever since he's been acting a bit out of character.' He frowned, fidgeting with one of the books on her counter top without really looking at it. 'I'm worried about the whole thing. About him. And her. So I'd like to come along and keep an eye on him. Understand?'

She did not understand, but decided not to question it. The sooner she could get rid of him, the better. Just looking at him was raising her blood pressure.

'Fair enough,' she said politely. 'Everyone has their reasons for wanting to come to the colouring book club.'

'So how do I start?'

'You turn up and start colouring. Nothing to it really.'

'But that's just it,' Matthew said. He leant forward conspiratorially. 'I've never actually … that is, I don't ever …' He watched her face. 'Would it be okay if I just sit there and watch?'

'Not do any colouring?'

'Exactly.'

She shook her head. 'No, I don't think it would be okay.'

Matthew looked startled by her blunt refusal. He tilted

his head to one side, considering her closely. God, those gorgeous eyes!

'So what you're saying is, if I come along to the club meeting, I'll have to do some colouring in, or else leave?'

'I'm afraid so.'

He continued to study her, his brows knit together. 'You don't like me,' Matthew said at last, as though deeply surprised by this discovery. 'Why not?'

Emma said nothing.

'There aren't many women who don't like me,' he remarked.

I bet, she thought savagely, but still said nothing.

He frowned, watching her. She could see him worrying away at the question, as though it meant a great deal to him to solve this mystery.

'Is it the flapjack thing again? Or something else?'

'I'm sorry, I've got a lot of work to do.' Emma turned away and began tapping busily at her keyboard, thereby deleting all the work she had previously done in a few strokes. She stared at the screen, which was now showing her an error message. 'Oh crap.'

Matthew had not moved.

'Look,' he said eventually, 'I'm serious about being worried. My dad's ... Well, he's different from other fathers. And I've got no idea what kind of woman this is he's met. For all I know, it could end in total disaster. For both of them.'

Total disaster.

She remembered again the humiliation of having this man witness her parents' departure only minutes after her announcement at the beach café. They had not been interested in listening to her stumbling explanation. Had not asked much beyond her mother's bewildered demand, 'Who's the father?' to which she had only been able to answer, 'I don't know.'

Her dad had been sympathetic. But her mum had dragged him away, saying she did not want to discuss it.

Not until Emma could tell them the 'truth'. As though she believed Emma had been lying.

So much for relying on her parents for some guidance on whether or not to continue with this unwanted pregnancy.

But at least now she knew where she stood.

Entirely alone.

Emma whipped round. 'And how is it any of your business what your dad chooses to do?'

His smile disappeared, his blue eyes suddenly serious. 'I can't explain. Maybe if I knew you better.'

She snorted.

Matthew shoved his hands into his jeans pockets. The movement stretched his clinging white T-shirt, outlining flat abs and that broad chest she had been ogling so pointlessly at the beach café.

'Okay, I'll come along to the next meeting and do some colouring-in. The same as everyone else. Satisfied?'

Was she satisfied?

Emma licked her lips, trying not to think about that question seriously.

She looked at the clock instead.

'It's my break time,' she said, and logged off her monitor. One of her supervisors walked past, glancing curiously at Matthew, and Emma was abruptly reminded of where she was, and her responsibilities as a member of the library staff. 'I'm sorry if I was sharp with you just now. But I'm … I'm a little tired, that's all. Not enough sleep last night.'

She did not want this man making a complaint about her attitude, or maybe about the club itself. It would not take much for library management to cancel the meetings; she knew they already looked down on colouring books as inferior to actual reading.

He looked taken aback, but nodded. 'Fair enough. Look, if you're going for your break, maybe I could walk out with you.'

Emma felt her heart thump at the suggestion, her breathing suddenly constricted. Good grief, she thought, reaching for her handbag under the counter. She found this man far too intriguing. And not just because he was physically attractive. There was something in his eyes …

'I'm only going to the staff room,' she told him, 'up on the third floor. But you can walk me to the lift.'

Matthew fell in beside her, matching his pace to hers.

'I really do want to apologise for intruding in your conversation at the beach,' he said after a moment, glancing at her sideways. 'I'm sorry if I embarrassed you.'

'It wasn't your fault.'

'I meant to come over after your parents left, apologise there and then. But by the time I was free, you'd gone.'

She had been so angry with him for witnessing her humiliation. Yet now she heard herself insisting that it really didn't matter.

'I guess they don't get on with your boyfriend.'

She looked at him, frowning.

He nodded to her left hand. 'No wedding ring. So I assumed …'

'No boyfriend either.'

'I see.'

She raised her eyebrows. 'I doubt it.'

'I'm sorry, I shouldn't have jumped to conclusions.' His voice deepened. 'Look, it's none of my business. But if you need a shoulder to cry on –'

'I beg your pardon?'

'Or just someone you can berate to make you feel better …' He grinned at her astonished glance. 'I'm at the beach café most days.'

'I'm here most days.'

He smiled appreciatively. 'Touché.' His gaze sought hers, and her stomach flipped over again in another of those disconcerting romance novel moves. 'Look, are you on Facebook?'

'Excuse me?'

He glanced at her name badge. 'Never mind.'

'Are you planning to stalk me online?

'Now there's an idea. Would you like that?'

Emma did not know how to respond. He was baiting her, of course. At least, she hoped so. She knew so little about this man.

'You're very odd,' she told him, her voice sharp.

'Thank you.'

They had reached the lift. He studied the sign that said, *Staff Only,* and grimaced. Like he knew he had been outplayed.

She pressed the call button, suddenly brisk. 'Well, this is me.'

'He's a fool, you know.'

She turned to him, searching his face. 'Who?'

'The one who isn't your boyfriend.'

The lift arrived with a shuddering clunk. The doors opened and Chloe emerged, dragging a trolley of books and journals for the Reference section.

'Hello, Emma,' Chloe said cheerfully. She smiled at Matthew, who smiled back in a perfunctory way and then continued looking at Emma again. Chloe's eyes widened as she studied him, as did her smile. She paused, then gave Emma an awful, conspiratorial wink. 'Going up for your break?'

Emma nodded but did not say anything, standing in gloomy silence until both Chloe and the book trolley had disappeared.

Oh, brilliant.

No doubt Chloe, one of the chief gossips on the library staff, believed the two of them were an item now. As in boyfriend/girlfriend.

'Matthew?' She pressed the call button again. The lift, which had been called away while she was still cringing over Chloe's wink, began to trundle back down to the ground floor. 'Can I ask you a favour? Please don't mention to anyone what you overheard at the café. My …

condition is not common knowledge.'

Looking round at him, Emma caught an odd look on his face.

Was Matthew sorry for her?

The thought infuriated her. She was not helpless and she did not need his pity. She had got herself into this mess; she would get herself out of it too.

'And it's never likely to be,' she added.

CHAPTER EIGHT

Emma ran up the stairs to her second floor flat.

'Hi, Emma, how are you?' her old neighbour Frank called after her, though she was sure all he could see were her disappearing legs.

'Fine, thanks. You?'

'Going and grumbling,' Frank replied, then puffed busily back through his doorway.

Emma smiled, letting herself into her own dimly-lit flat. Though bedsit would be its technical description, she considered, glancing about the place. The one-room flat was so small, her dad had once joked it was too small even to swing a mouse in, let alone a cat. It was not the wonderful living space she had envisaged when she first chose to leave home and set up on her own. Yet Emma had chosen it within seconds of walking in with the agent, even though she had just come from viewing three far larger and more comfortable apartments.

She had fallen in love with its brash floral wallpaper and the view from the window, which looked towards the local park, not to mention the very reasonable rent. It had been perfect for her needs at the time.

There would be no room here for a baby though.

Besides which, her tenancy agreement absolutely forbade children. Even very small ones whose only real daily needs were hugs and generous helpings of milk.

'Impossible,' she reminded herself, trying not to look in the mirror as she stripped off her work clothes. 'Simply impossible.'

She dragged out some old jeans and a light blue sweatshirt. Something casual and comfortable, as far from professional as possible: her jeans had little splits in the knees, and her sweatshirt was faded from too many washes. She liked to keep a clear demarcation between work and home, and clothes was an easy way to do that.

Her jeans were tighter than usual at the waist. She frowned, struggling with the zip, then stopped abruptly.

She was getting fatter. But not through too many cakes and lattes in her break times.

It had to be the baby. What other explanation could there be?

She stripped off the jeans again and pulled on some black leggings instead. The material was stretchy, more forgiving of the tiny rounding of her belly, barely perceptible in the mirror yet real enough to make her jeans too tight to fasten.

'Damn.'

Though she probably was eating too much. It was easier for a woman to put on weight when she was pregnant, Emma was sure she had read that somewhere.

'No more cakes.'

She pulled the sweatshirt down over her belly, and instantly felt better. Out of sight, out of mind.

If only, she thought drily, and sat down at her computer. She checked her private email address first. Nothing exciting. Then she got out a notebook and pen, and put it beside the screen. It was time she made a proper effort to track him down, the father of her child. But where to start looking? She knew so little about him, just as he had known almost nothing about her.

'I must have been mad,' she said to herself, but began to list the few things she could remember about him.

He was out there somewhere. And she was going to find him.

But her fingers slowed on the keys as she began her Google search with the bare facts available.

What if she eventually managed to find him, and he wanted her to keep the baby? Worse, what if she discovered he was some dreadful person – a criminal, perhaps, or a serial adulterer – but then could not get rid of him, because of the baby she was carrying?

Perhaps it would be better if she never tracked him down.

Guilt assailed her instantly.

He could be a perfectly nice man, and just as confused as her by their insta-romance that night. He deserved to know he had fathered a child.

Didn't he?

Painstakingly, Emma searched Google Images using "Ibiza" and the dates of her holiday first. No one even remotely similar to her one-night-stand turned up over four or five pages of holiday pictures. Then she tried again, this time entering the name of the resort she had been staying at. Nothing. She also tried the same searches, but alongside the first names of the passing acquaintances she had hung out with on the beach. This was just in case they'd posted holiday snaps to Facebook.

One by one at first, and then together, she typed in: Talli, Kim, Sandra, Paul, Nazeem and "Ibiza".

She didn't know surnames. Had taken no photos herself. It had been one of those wild, anonymous escapes from everyday life, she thought, grimacing at the useless search results.

No names, no details, no responsibilities. And no bloody contraception either.

A sponsored advert came up in the sidebar: Private Detectives.

She stared at it, tempted.

Then she moved on, putting the possibility to the back of her mind. She did not have enough money as it was. Paying a professional agency to track down this guy would only strain her already meagre resources. Nor did she want the embarrassment of explaining to a complete stranger exactly what she had done in Ibiza, and why she needed this man found so quickly.

There was a message for her on Facebook, and a new friendship request. She clicked the little red flag, her heart leaping.

Could it be the father of her child?

But her heart sank at the smiling photo that accompanied the friendship request. It was only Matthew, the guy from the café.

'How the hell did he find me?'

Then she remembered him looking at her name badge at the library. He still wanted them to become friends on Facebook, she realised, even though she had given him the brush-off at work. Persistent devil that he was.

She glanced at his message.

Let me take you out after the next meeting. You choose where. No strings attached. It would be good to have a longer chat.

Was this about his dad again? Or about the colouring book club?

He fancied her.

She wanted to deny it, but she had seen that look in his eyes. And she herself had felt something in return. She wasn't sure what. Except that she instinctively liked him.

She stared at his photo again. Matthew looked friendly and uncomplicated, no dark secrets behind that open smile. And she envied him his close relationship with his dad. It was sweet of him to be looking out for Boris, making sure he didn't get hurt. All the same, it was impossible. Completely and utterly impossible. In her situation, she could not be starting a new relationship. She should not even contemplate starting one. Yet here she was, doing precisely that.

It would be good to have a longer chat.

Unsure, she hovered her cursor over the Confirm or Deny button. She ought to ignore his friendship request. Or deny it. She was being stupid.

But his eyes …

Emma hit Confirm, and they were friends.

Just like that.

She looked at the screen message confirming their online friendship. Then she banged her forehead on the desk, groaning under her breath. She was such an unholy mess of contradictions. Get rid of the baby, look after the baby. Find the father of her child, ignore his existence. Now here she was, getting involved with a good-looking man while perfectly aware that it was impossible for her to get involved with anyone.

She could not bear the circular argument in her head any longer, so distracted herself by googling 'Colouring Lovers'.

To her horror, she got page after page of porn results. Smiling naked couples covered in tattoos.

'Bloody hell.'

Emma deleted that search and tried trawling some Facebook groups instead. There were a few online groups for discussing and recommending colouring books, but none where people could actually meet up in person. So she took ten minutes to set up a local group page for her Colouring Book Club, with all the meeting information, and then typed in contact details for the library. No photos yet, but she would take some at the next meeting, if people didn't mind, and post one up for her cover page.

Emma smiled, leaning back in her seat to admire her handiwork. She was quite excited by how popular her colouring book club had proved so far. Not the most ambitious project ever, but it certainly took her mind off the Other Thing.

Then someone knocked at her door.

Emma jumped up, startled.

Who on earth?

She had sudden ludicrous visions of finding the father of her child on the doorstep, having miraculously sought her out, ready to help her unravel this problem.

But it was only another of her neighbours from downstairs, Dita, whose very round belly proclaimed her to be in the last stages of pregnancy herself.

Dita smiled at Emma, then glanced past her at the computer screen. 'So sorry to disturb you. Were you working?'

'Not at all,' Emma said cheerfully, opening the door wider. She always had time for Dita. 'Just messing about on Facebook, you know. Please, come in.'

'No, it's fine. I only came up to ask if I may borrow your hoover again. Mine's still refusing to turn on.'

'Of course. Let me carry it downstairs for you.'

'There's no need, really.'

But Emma insisted. 'How long now?' she asked, a little breathlessly, when they reached the bottom of the stairs. She nodded towards Dita's huge tummy under her bright orange top. 'I don't want to be rude, but that looks vast. Like you're ready to pop.'

'Another fortnight. And thank goodness for that, I'm so sick of being pregnant.' Dita grinned at Emma's expression, then stretched out her back as though it was aching. 'But you know, babies don't run on a schedule. She could make an appearance any day now. Or even hang on another few weeks.'

'She?'

'We asked at the scan. It's a girl.'

Emma could not speak. She smiled though, finally managing to say, 'That's lovely. You must be so excited. Well, just give me a shout when you've finished with the hoover.'

'I'll get Dan to bring it up to you, please don't worry. Thanks, Emma, you've been very kind.'

'What's the landlord said about having a baby here?'

Dita shook her head. 'We have to move out. But not until the baby's born. Dan's looking for another place now. Somewhere with two bedrooms.'

'Good luck, I hope you find somewhere nicer than this.'

Her neighbour laughed. 'Unlikely,' she said with a shrug, yet did not seem too bothered by the prospect. 'I'm giving up work for at least the first six months. To spend time at home with the baby. So our income is going to drop massively, even after benefits.'

'Doesn't that bother you?'

'No, I'm looking forward to it.' Dita patted her tummy. 'Can't wait to meet my daughter.'

Emma watched the pregnant woman waddle back into her flat, then she climbed slowly back up the stairs to her own grim bedsit.

A girl.

Up until now, she had been thinking of the baby inside her as an 'it'. No gender, no name, no identity. It had felt easier that way. Easier to stay detached, to be more logical about what lay ahead. But the way Dita had spoken just now, rubbing her swollen tummy with every evidence of motherly love, even though the baby had not yet made an appearance …

Can't wait to meet my daughter.

Dita's baby was a girl. She would probably grow up to be someone like her mother. To help people or build things or invent stuff or run an organisation.

Dita's child would have a chance.

She was on the verge of tears now, everything in turmoil inside her. It felt like really bad PMT.

Emma shut her door quietly and threw herself on her bed. She closed her eyes, her mind clenched like a fist around something both terrible and precious.

She was pregnant too, but alone, without even knowing the man who had put this life inside her. When she found out, part of her had assumed the answer to this dilemma would be a simple yes/no situation. But this question was a billion times more complicated than she had initially thought. And it was rather late to be realising that the baby inside her was not an "it" but already a "he" or a "she". That the tiny creature making it hard for her to fasten her jeans might be silent and invisible, but was already a person.

She thought fleetingly about adoption.

But that would mean going through with the pregnancy, with everyone knowing that she was expecting, but then handing over her baby to a stranger at the end of it.

If only there was someone she could talk to in confidence about all this. Someone outside the situation who could advise her. She might have asked Dita under other circumstances, but she did not want to have to face her neighbour every day if she later took the heart-rending decision to end this unwanted pregnancy.

And if only her mum and dad were not so disgusted by what they saw as her promiscuous behaviour. They were not even open to a conversation at the moment. They would probably come round, in time. Maybe a few months down the line. But she needed someone now. Urgently. Before it was too late.

The cursor blinked on the computer screen.

She sat up and stared at it.

Then she hurried to the computer and clicked back to her Facebook message screen.

Let me take you out after the next meeting. You choose where. No strings attached. It would be good to have a longer chat.

She read Matthew's words through several times, then replied briefly, *Okay, how about The Strand pub? Just for an hour after the meeting.*

Emma sent the reply before she could change her mind.

'Too late now,' she told herself, though her heart was

thudding loudly and she felt distinctly jittery.

Getting up, Emma wandered to the window to stare out at the park. Her favourite view. Fresh green leaves, trees in blossom. She did not know why on earth she was fretting about this guy. Yes, she liked Matthew. Far too much, truth be told. But she had regained her self-control after the insanity of Ibiza; she did not need to act on her impulses in the same way.

Besides, this was not a date. It would not be even remotely romantic. It was a drink with a new acquaintance. A drink and maybe a chat about her ... options.

What harm could it do?

CHAPTER NINE

'You feeling better now, Crystal?' her mum asked solicitously on the way up the library stairs. Her hand gripped Crystal by the elbow, supporting her up the last few steps like she was an old lady. 'Not in any more pain?'

Crystal bit her lip. Damn her feeble body for playing up at precisely the wrong time.

They were late to the colouring club meeting again. Worse still, it looked like everyone else was already there.

But she had not been able to leave the house any earlier. A terrible headache had been followed by stomach cramps, and although the cramps had eased off somewhat, she was still aching all over. She ought to be lying down with a well-wrapped hot water bottle on her belly, if she could have stood the boredom of another evening spent in front of the television. But it always upset her mum to think of her in pain, so Crystal kept all that to herself.

'I'm okay, don't fuss.'

'Because I brought extra supplies in my bag,' her mum hissed as they pushed open the door.

'Mum, I don't need anything.' Crystal made a face. 'If I take another pill, I'll start to rattle.'

Her mum gave her arm a quick squeeze. 'That's the

spirit, love. But you'll let me know at once if … if you need to go home, won't you? No point suffering in silence.'

Emma had turned as the door opened, looking at them curiously. She must have caught the last few words of their whispered conversation.

'You not feeling a hundred percent, Crystal?' Emma's smile faded as she assessed Crystal's stiff stance, her brows crunching up with genuine concern. 'I'm so sorry to hear that. Nothing serious, I hope.'

Crystal did not know whether to laugh or cry.

'Really, it's nothing,' she told the room firmly, as every head turned in her direction. 'Just a tummy ache.'

Emma's eyes widened. 'Right,' she said faintly, then pulled out a chair for Crystal to join the others at the colouring table. 'I know how that feels.'

I doubt it, Crystal thought, but managed a smile in return. Emma was kind and meant well. But she had no idea how serious Crystal's condition was, and hopefully never would.

'Let's hope it soon passes,' Emma continued, helping her sympathetically towards the table. 'Come and see what's arrived. New colouring books for the club.'

'Oh Emma, they look brilliant.' Fiona was already poring over the new colouring books with her usual zeal. 'But wait until you see what I've got here.'

She dragged some new books of her own from her capacious handbag, and waved them at the company. 'The colouring books I ordered have arrived too. One came all the way from New Zealand. Look at this.' Fiona thumbed through to her favourite section. 'Koalas chewing twigs. So cute.'

Emma grinned at the amusing picture. 'Thanks, Fiona.'

'Fifi, please.'

'Of course, sorry. I meant Fifi.'

Crystal gave an inward groan, sinking onto the seat Emma was holding out for her. Her mum meant well too, but her over-enthusiasm could be a little grating at times. She glanced round the table, still curious about the other members of this unusual club. She herself would never have turned up to a colouring book club if her mum had not insisted on dragging her along. To 'keep her mind off things,' as Fiona put it.

One of the strangest things was the number of men who had turned up for that first meeting. She would never have thought grown men would be interested in colouring-in pictures. But as she did a quick head count, she realised not all the men had come back. There had been a quiet bloke in the corner last time. He had not turned up this time.

And Jack was not there either.

But the tattooed Boris was there again, and this time he had brought someone with him. Clearly his son, she thought wryly.

They weren't exactly identical – the younger man still had a full head of hair, for a start – but they were both muscular and well-built, their eyes a similar shade of blue, and they both shared the same jutting chin.

The younger man caught her eye, and then leaned across the table to shake her hand. There was something meaningful about his grip. As though he had noted and sympathised with her embarrassment over her mum's behaviour.

'Matthew,' he introduced himself with a smile. 'Boris is my dad. When he told me about this club, I thought I'd better come along too. Keep him out of trouble.'

Behind him, Emma cleared her throat. 'Shall we start?' she asked abruptly, and drew up a chair without acknowledging that he had spoken.

It occurred to Crystal that Emma was uncomfortable about Matthew's presence, to judge by the way she avoided even looking at him as she reached for the pile of new colouring books. 'I've been doing some research about colouring and shading techniques, and discovered some expert tips that might be worth sharing.'

'Now that sounds promising,' Fiona gushed, and smiled at Crystal. 'We total newbies could do with some tips, couldn't we?'

Emma flicked through one of the new books, still looking troubled. 'Well, I don't want to bore anyone. But we could have a chat about technique before we start. If that's all right with everyone.'

Fiona immediately said, 'Oh yes, please.'

Crystal glanced at the door, wondering firstly if Jack had decided never to come again, and secondly if his no-show was connected to the cold way she had dismissed him last time they spoke.

She tried to ignore her disappointment at his absence.

Boris nodded, saying gruffly, 'That's an excellent idea, thank you.'

His son twirled a royal blue felt tip in his hand, his gaze on Emma's averted face. 'I agree,' Matthew said, apparently unaware that he was being ignored. Or perhaps not caring. There was an ironic edge to his voice that suggested the latter. 'Take this felt tip. I can just about work out which end does what, but how to apply it to paper without scribbling like a toddler is a mystery. So any tips would be gratefully received.'

'Okay,' Emma said, still not looking at Matthew. Her smile was strained now. 'I'll start with some basic techniques, in that case. For instance, does anyone know which part of a picture we should start colouring first?'

Everyone started to talk at once.

Crystal did not join in the discussion, but listened for the sound of feet on the stairs instead. But there was no sound from outside the very firmly closed door. She watched the hands of the clock move inexorably round while Emma demonstrated various shading techniques, first on a whiteboard and then in one of the new books she had provided.

Where the hell was Jack?

She was such a fool.

Why on earth did she care that Jack had not turned up at the meeting? What was wrong with her? Was this guilt? Or wounded vanity?

She could have screamed in frustration. This was so ridiculous. She had more or less told him to get lost, and now she was put out because he was not at the colouring club meeting? She had to get a grip on her fantasies. Because a fantasy was precisely what this was.

She was seriously ill, near the top of the transplant list. She could die at any minute. She could not waste what were potentially her last few months of life worrying about some guy who might or might not have been hurt by her rejection.

'Crystal?'

She blinked, looking round at her mum. 'Sorry?'

'You've been tapping your pen really noisily,' Fiona whispered, leaning across with a frown.

Crystal stared at the pen in her hand, only now realising that she had been banging it on the table for some minutes now, her drawing forgotten.

'Sorry.'

Her mum put a reassuring hand on her arm. 'You sure you're okay? I won't be cross if you'd rather leave.'

'No, I'm just …'

The door swung open, and she turned, startled.

It was Jack.

'Sorry I'm late,' he said, a touch curtly, and shrugged out of his leather jacket.

She almost recoiled as he pulled out the chair next to her and sat down, his thigh brushing hers.

He glanced at her. 'Crystal.'

'Jack.'

What else was there to say?

Plenty, apparently, she thought as her mum launched helpfully into a mini-explanation of everything they had discussed so far.

It was a shock to see him again, she realised. Not least because she had forgotten the effect he had on her nerves. No, not her nerves. Her whole body. She had not been feeling too bad as the colouring buzz kicked in, her mind finding a little peace as she coloured. But now, she felt in shreds. Like a rag blowing in the wind.

He was her Kryptonite.

But that would make her Superman, wouldn't it? And she was no superhero. Quite the opposite, in fact.

He pushed a packet of watercolour pencils towards her. 'Care to share?'

'These are lovely.' She fingered the expensive-looking packet, feeling pencil-envy. 'Are you sure?'

'Of course.'

She turned to a new page in her book and tried one of the salmon-pink pencils out on a flamingo. It was rich and deep and so soft on the page. 'Oh my goodness.'

'Better than felt tips,' he said, 'aren't they?'

'No contest.'

He handed her a deep blue pencil for the lake. 'Here, try this.'

It felt so good in her hand. Thick and slightly stubby, yet somehow the perfect weight too. It filled her palm exactly.

The blue was impressively deep – and not at all grainy, which she had half expected.

'Oh,' she said.

His gaze devoured her face, the curve of her throat. 'You like it?'

'Very much.'

'Take whatever you want.'

She was so tempted. 'But what about you?' She shot a swift look at his colouring book. The book had been opened to the intricate drawing of a peony bloom; it was all gorgeous petals and folds, spilling luxuriously over the whole page. 'That's going to take a lot of pencil. I don't want to monopolise your pink and red shades.'

'Maybe I'll go with yellow instead. Yellow and deep gold.'

She looked at him wonderingly. 'Pink would suit it better.'

'You take the pinks for your flamingos, I don't need them.' As though to underline his point, Jack pulled all the yellow and gold pencils out of the packet, lining them up neatly in front of his colouring book. 'No, I insist. Choosing less obvious colours can make the end-effect more unique.'

She selected another of his expensive pencils and began work, smiling. 'Emma was just saying that.'

His smile was crooked. 'It's mostly common sense.'

'And artistic gift.'

He looked at her drawing, the subtle shading she had already begun on the trees behind the lake. 'You certainly have that,' he told her. 'That looks so good, almost like a painting. Are you going to double-layer your shading?'

'You think I should?'

He tilted a thick gold pencil in his large hand and started to shade the outer petals of the peony. 'It gives the picture more depth.'

Emma came over to look at what they were both doing. The librarian murmured her praise of both pictures, but leant closely over Jack's peony.

Too closely, in Crystal's opinion.

A loose strand of hair fell over Emma's face as she bent over. She scooped it back behind one ear, seeming to blush slightly as she did so. 'Oh Jack, that's lovely.' Her smile was almost flirtatious. 'I can see someone's been doing research on shading technique since our last meeting.'

Jack grinned up at her. 'I must admit, I did print out a few sheets on technique from the internet.'

'It shows. And what a bold choice, going for yellow.'

'Thank you, Emma.'

Crystal bent assiduously to her own colouring, but felt

her teeth grind together. It was stupid, really. She could not go out with Jack. But she did not like the idea of anyone else making a play for him either.

'Beautiful flamingos,' Emma told her briefly, before moving round the table to admire Fiona's hedgehog buried in lovingly detailed autumn leaves.

Whatever.

Valiantly, she suppressed the very real urge to snap at the librarian. It must not look or sound like she was jealous. That would be too embarrassing. And so pointless too. Crystal glanced across at the others, and caught an odd expression on Matthew's face. Matthew had stopped colouring and was watching Emma instead as she talked to Fiona, his dark eyes intent on her face. Abruptly he glanced at Jack, and his gaze hardened. Like he was angry.

Or jealous?

She could have laughed out loud. Except it was not really funny.

'You said we ought to think about choosing unusual colours,' her mum was saying, pointing to the lurid green and red stripes she had given her unfortunate hedgehog. 'What do you think, Emma?'

'Erm ...'

For once, the librarian was lost for words.

'I thought a light blue for the autumn leaves would make a striking contrast. But should I go for lilac instead? Or maybe this shade of purple?' Fiona continued, holding up a deep purple pen for inspection. 'Too much?'

Suddenly, Emma straightened up. She gulped, then clamped a hand to her mouth, her expression mortified. 'Sorry,' she said, and dashed from the room.

The group sat in stunned silence, listening to Emma stumbling down the stairs, the door slowly closing behind her.

'Oh dear.' Fiona looked down at her colouring with a dubious expression. 'I think my hedgehog made her sick.'

Without a word, Matthew pushed back his chair and

followed Emma swiftly from the room. He was frowning.

What on earth is going on? Crystal wondered.

'Now, don't take on, it weren't your hedgehog what did that to the poor girl,' Boris reassured her mum, though he too had been eyeing her lurid creation with some uncertainty. 'I expect she ate something what disagreed with her. Bad eggs for breakfast, maybe.'

'You sure?'

'Course I'm sure, Fifi.'

Then he winked at her, and Fiona blushed.

Her mum actually blushed.

The undisguised intimacy of this exchange made Crystal's eyes widen. Was the old sea-dog falling in love with her mum? It must be impossible. And yet Fiona had not come back from her surfing lesson with him for hours. Surely they had not …

Jack leant back in his chair. He was gazing at the closed door, his brow furrowed. 'Perhaps you ought to go after her too,' he said quietly to Crystal.

'Me?'

He looked at her.

'Right, yes.' She stood up and closed her colouring book. Her mum looked across at her, surprised. 'I'm going to check if Emma's all right. Be right back.'

It was no use explaining to Jack that she was not particularly fit herself. That the trek up and down stairs might do her more damage than it had done poor Emma. The librarian probably only had a touch of food poisoning, like Boris had suggested. But then Crystal told herself off for being unhelpful. Perhaps Emma was genuinely unwell, and needed another woman there. It was late and the rest of the library, though still open, was always quiet at this time of the evening. Emma was probably alone in the ladies. Unless Matthew had followed her in there.

Matthew had not followed her inside. He was outside the ladies, pacing up and down, his face worried.

He turned hurriedly as Crystal approached. 'Oh thank

God. She's not come out yet, and I didn't like to knock.'

'Don't worry.'

She pushed into the ladies, and saw the end cubicle was closed. 'Emma? It's Crystal. Do you need any help?'

There was a muffled reply.

'I'm sorry, I didn't quite catch —'

The toilet flushed, and then the cubicle door opened. Emma emerged, her cheeks paper-white, eyes slightly bloodshot, her hair dishevelled.

It was obvious that she had been sick.

Crystal knew how it felt when people intruded on her illness. But Emma had been well at the last meeting. Glowing, almost. So perhaps this was indeed food poisoning.

Or something worse.

She felt guilty at how she had dismissed Emma's dash from the room. Nobody knew she was ill. So perhaps Emma was in a bad condition too.

'Do you need a doctor?'

'No,' Emma said, and bent over a sink to splash her face with cold water. 'There, that's better.'

Crystal passed her some paper hand towels.

'Thanks.'

'You sure I can't call someone? One of the other librarians, perhaps?'

'God, no.' Drying her face and hands, Emma stared at her in the mirror. Her eyes were very wide, her expression frightened. 'Please don't say anything.'

'Of course not.'

'Promise me.'

'Cross my heart and hope to die.'

'Thank you.'

'Listen, I won't say a word to anyone. You can trust me. But you look like you need some help.'

'I know it looks bad, but I don't need a doctor. This is perfectly normal. I was only sick because I'm ...' Emma steadied herself against the sink, then straightened, turning to face Crystal. Her chin lifted, a slight colour returning to her pale cheeks as she finished, 'I'm pregnant.'

Crystal felt her mouth sagging, and hurriedly closed it. That was not what she had expected to hear. She nodded. 'Goodness, congratulations.' Then saw Emma's misery, and added, 'Or not?'

Emma threw the damp paper towels in the swing bin. 'The news has not been exactly welcome, no.'

'I'm so sorry.' How awful, she was thinking. 'Look, I know it's none of my business. But is there anything I can do to help?'

'You could help me find out who the father is.'

CHAPTER TEN

Crystal had been shocked by Emma's request for help, and not sure she was the right person to ask even if she'd been keen to help. Could Emma be serious? Did she really not know who the father of her child was?

All the same, she agreed to meet Emma one afternoon soon, when they could get their schedules to coincide with a dry, sunny day. She badly needed a friend. In fact, it sounded like they *both* needed a friend.

'We could go swimming together,' Crystal had suggested. 'To be honest, I'm not sure I can help you find this guy. But I'll do whatever I can.'

'Thanks.' Emma hesitated. 'Wait, swimming? You mean in the sea?'

'Why not? I love the beach, don't you?'

Emma looked unsure.

'If you ask me, you're too pale,' she told Emma firmly. 'You could do with some sun, sea and sand.'

'Too pale? Have you looked in a mirror lately? You're doing a pretty good impersonation of a vampire.'

Crystal grimaced, remembering that awkward exchange in the ladies' toilets. Her skin was very pale at the moment, thanks to her condition, and Emma had clearly not been fooled by her rambling explanation of a low iron count.

Emma deserved the truth. She had taken a risk in baring her own soul to Crystal. And she would get the truth. Just not yet.

But when she saw the librarian slip away with Matthew at the end of the colouring club meeting, the two of them talking quietly, head-to-head, Crystal had to hide her astonishment.

She wondered if Matthew knew about the baby.

Also getting up to leave, Crystal spotted her mum whispering in Boris's ear at the refreshment table. He was listening with apparent fascination, a half-smile on his normally gruff face.

'Mum?' Crystal packed away her books and colouring tools.

'In a minute, love.'

She tried not to catch Jack's eye. But it was hopeless. The man was determined to get some time alone with her.

'Can we talk?' he asked quietly.

'I don't think that would be a very good idea.'

Jack raised his eyebrows. 'Can I be the judge of that? You must know I have questions. You can't just throw a lie at me like that –'

'What lie?'

'You know what you said, Crystal. Or did it mean so little to you that you've already forgotten?' He leant closer, lowering his voice so the others in the room would not overhear. 'You said you didn't find me attractive.'

'No, I said you weren't my type.'

Jack tilted his head to one side, regarding her steadily.

She looked away, flustered by that look. How the hell was he able to get under her skin so easily?

'Anyway, it wasn't a lie.'

'Fibber,' he said softly.

Crystal turned and glared at her mother and Boris. She badly needed to escape from Jack, and as soon as possible. But how? The older man had an arm round her mother's waist now, and far from pushing him away, Fiona was actually giggling.

It was definitely time to get out of here.

Since her mum's car was on the blink again, they had taken a taxi cab into the town centre. So unless they wanted to walk all the way home to the guesthouse, she needed to call the taxi firm and order a return cab.

'Mum,' she said loudly.

Her mother sighed and looked round at her, obviously annoyed at being interrupted. 'What is it, Crystal?' She sounded as petulant as a teenager. 'What's the matter?'

'The meeting's finished, in case you hadn't noticed. It's time to go.' She fished her phone out of her bag. 'Shall I call us a taxi home?'

Boris muttered something in Fiona's ear.

'Um, Boris wants to take me to the pub,' Fiona told her apologetically. 'He's got his van outside. Can we drop you back at the guesthouse?'

Crystal stared, lowering the mobile.

She did not know what to say.

Ordinarily she would have been delighted that her mother was showing an interest in another man since her acrimonious divorce. But under the circumstances, with Jack watching her so closely and her stomach turning somersaults, the last thing she wanted was to deal with these two lovebirds on the way home.

Their giggles and secret whispers had already left her feeling uncomfortable. She could only imagine what they might get up to in the dark interior of a car.

'I'll take Crystal home,' Jack offered calmly. He took Crystal's arm as though she would have no possible objection to the plan. 'You two go ahead. Enjoy yourselves.'

'What? No.' Crystal extricated herself from his grip with some difficulty. 'Thanks, but I'm happy to walk.'

'You can't walk home by yourself.' Her mum was shocked.

'Don't worry, I won't let her walk home,' Jack assured them all, and took Crystal's arm again.

Crystal glared at him. Fuming at his highhanded behaviour, she unlinked her arm from his for a second time.

'I like walking.'

Frowning, Boris took a step back from her mother. His shaven head gleamed under the ceiling spotlights; he ran a tattooed hand over the smooth skin, looking pensive. 'Hey look, Fifi, it's no problem. Perhaps we should hook up at the pub another evening. Sounds like a bad time, yeah?'

Fiona caught her breath, looking at him. There was hurt in her eyes, but a sad kind of resignation too. 'If you want.'

Oh bloody hell.

'No, no,' Crystal said sharply, and made a grab for Jack's arm, dragging him towards her. 'I've changed my mind. You two go to the pub, and Jack can … take me to dinner. I haven't tried that new Indian restaurant yet. I do love a nice curry.'

Her mother was looking at her, uncertain. 'Oh darling, I don't know. You and curry …'

'I'll be fine.'

Jack did not waste any more time. 'Okay then, see you both later,' he told Boris and Fiona, nodded to the other two women still chatting in the corner, then walked out with Crystal on his arm.

'Hold on.'

Crystal turned in the doorway, surprised. Her mum had come charging after her with an intense look in her eyes.

'Give us a minute, would you?' her mum asked Jack with strained politeness.

He nodded without any argument and walked down the stairs alone, his hands in his pockets. She watched him wander slowly across the lobby below, head bent as though studying his own shoes.

'All right, he can't hear us. Now what is this about?'

Crystal stared at her mum. 'I'm not upset about you and Boris, if that's what you think. I mean, Boris wouldn't be my taste. But if you're interested, go for it.'

Her mum raised her eyebrows. 'Good, because I do like Boris, and I am going for it.'

'Enjoy.'

'The reason I came after you ... Well, it's none of my business either. But are you leaving with Jack because of me? So as not to make up a threesome?'

'A *threesome*?'

'On the way home.' Fiona looked horrified. 'What did you think I meant?'

'Oh, right. Erm, nothing.' Crystal suppressed her grin. 'No, of course not. I've decided to talk to Jack properly, that's all.'

Fiona's eyes narrowed on her face. 'Properly?'

'I need to tell him the truth.'

'Oh no, that's not a very good idea. You can't tell him, Crystal. Not yet anyway. Let the poor boy get to know you better first.' Her mum shook her head. 'There's no harm in avoiding the truth.'

But Crystal's mind was made up. 'I can't lie to him, Mum. It wouldn't be fair.'

'It's not lying.'

'It would be lying *by omission*.' Crystal kissed her mum on the cheek. 'Look, don't worry about it. You go off to the pub with Boris. Enjoy yourselves. I'll see you later.'

'But –'

'Please, let me do this my way. Jack's a nice bloke. He needs to know what he's getting into with me.' Crystal smiled at her mother, though inside she was crying. 'He deserves the truth.'

The Indian restaurant was down a side-street in the town centre. At first she thought they'd had a power cut. But apparently the candlelight was mood lighting. The walls were decorated with intricate Indian art and old photographs from the days of the Raj. It was an intimate space, and the sensual Indian music coming through the ceiling speakers was pitched just low enough not to be intrusive.

'This way please, madam, sir.' The waiter led them to an alcove table with gorgeous-looking leather bench seats. Crystal slid in first, and Jack sat opposite. 'Can I get you any drinks?'

She ordered a glass of sparkling water, and saw Jack's surprised glance.

'You don't want wine?'

'No thanks, water is fine.'

He ordered a half pint of Indian lager, and waited until the man had gone away before leaning forward. 'Are you feeling under the weather?' He sounded concerned. 'I would have taken you straight home if you'd told me.'

'I'll survive.'

Jack frowned, but did not argue.

She felt horribly awkward, and could not look at him. If she did, all the words would tumble out, and probably upside-down and in the wrong order. Instead she studied the pictures above their table. One looked remarkably erotic.

Inevitably Jack noticed what she was looking at, and looked too. He raised his eyebrows. 'Bit racy, that picture.'

'Is that man putting his …? Oh my goodness.'

Jack smiled, watching as she began rearranging the cutlery in a nervous manner. 'Talking of goodness, your mum and Boris … I didn't see that one coming.'

'He took her surfing the other week.'

'Sly dog.'

'That's one way of putting it.' She glanced at the erotic Indian picture again, then hurriedly away. 'Though I'm fine with it. She may be my mum but she's a grown woman, and they're both divorced. Why shouldn't he take her out?'

'It sounds like you're trying hard to convince yourself that's true.'

Crystal met his gaze, suddenly annoyed. 'My mum likes Boris. Nothing else matters.'

'What did she say to you, just before we left?'

'None of your business.'

'Warned you off me, did she?'

Her eyes widened on his face. 'No, of course not.'

'So why chase after you like that? It was obviously something urgent. I saw her face.' His eyes brooded on a couple at the next table, who were eating silently without looking at each other. 'Fiona thinks I'm not good enough for you, is that it? Or maybe it's because of my girlfriend's death? Does your mother suspect I had something to do with that?'

She was shocked. 'God, no.'

'Because not a day goes by that I don't think of her. Remember her smile, the way we were together. Wish she was still alive.'

Crystal studied his averted face. 'If that's true, what are you doing here? With me?'

'Good question.'

She did not know how to answer that. His fist had clenched on the dessert spoon. 'Have you changed your mind about dinner?' she asked quietly. 'Would you rather I left?'

'No.' His voice was deep and furious. 'You must know I'm interested in you. That I do find you attractive.'

Her heart was hammering. 'I had a vague idea, yes.'

'Making it obvious, am I?'

'I'm sorry I said you weren't my type.'

His head remained bent, but he stilled. 'It was a lie?'

Crystal whispered, 'Yes.'

'Thank God. I didn't think you were telling the truth. I was getting all these signals off you, but then you were saying the complete opposite.'

'Maybe I'm just a contrary bitch.'

'Yes, that's a distinct possibility.' Jack smiled. But then the smile faded and he shook his head. 'Bloody hell, no.

What's the matter with me? There are so many things I want to say to you tonight, but I keep tripping over my own tongue.'

She took a deep breath. 'Funny thing is, there are some things I need to tell you too. Things you ought to hear before you decide if you want to go any further with this ... this relationship.'

Raising his head, Jack stared at her. 'Such as?'

'Such as, I'm dying.'

'Oh God, I don't believe it.'

'You don't believe what?' Emma turned to see what Matthew was staring at across the crowded pub. Her eyes widened. 'Good grief. Isn't that –?'

'Yes, that's my dad. With his new squeeze.'

'But that's Crystal's mum, from the colouring book club.' She was surprised. 'That's his new girlfriend?'

'Fiona.'

'Apparently she prefers Fifi.'

He looked round at her apologetically. 'Listen, I didn't know they'd be here tonight. I'm ever so sorry.'

'No need. I think your dad's funny.'

'Good to know somebody does.'

Boris had spotted them too, and was clearly aware that he was being observed. He raised his pint glass in a kind of wry salute. Beside him, Fiona smiled uncertainly, patted her hair, and then looked away.

No doubt she was as embarrassed to be seen out with Boris as Matthew was to be spotted by his dad.

'Great minds think alike,' Emma said.

'What do you mean?'

'For starters, you both chose this pub for tonight's drink.'

Matthew grinned. 'Not that much of a shock coincidence. It's our local. We only live a few hundred yards down the road.'

'Ah, that explains everything,' she said, and too late

heard the wry drawl in her voice. Like she cared.

He frowned a question at her.

Emma should have kept quiet. She did not want him to think she was jealous. 'The barmaid has been ogling you ever since we walked in,' she said, 'not to mention giving me daggers. I expect she's had her eye on you for ages. And now you're in here with another woman.'

He turned, gazing at the pretty, red-haired barmaid in confusion. 'Who, Becky? No, you must be mistaken. She's already got a boyfriend.'

'He should be worried, then.'

Matthew looked back at her, surprised, as though trying to work out if she was joking or not. Then he laughed. 'Women.'

'Little darlings, aren't we?'

'Hell hath no fury.'

'Save it, I'm neither scorned nor furious.' She knocked back her fruit juice with a grimace. 'But I do miss dry white wine.'

His expression sobered at once. He studied her face. 'So you're going ahead with it? The pregnancy?'

'Hush.' Emma glared at him, then glanced round the crowded pub. They were standing near the fruit machines, all lights and clicks and bells. It was very noisy, and probably nobody in the immediate vicinity could hear a word they were saying. But she was not yet ready for her pregnancy to be common knowledge. 'Please don't use the P word.'

'Sorry.'

'Anyway, I didn't say that.'

'Sorry,' he repeated.

'No need to apologise.'

'Sorry.'

She raised her eyebrows at him, and Matthew made a contrite face.

'Sorry, it just slipped out. Shit, s … sorry.' He rolled his eyes and slapped himself on the forehead several times.

'Idiot, see?'

'I didn't like to comment.'

'Well, anyway,' he continued easily, before she was really aware what he was asking, 'are you going ahead with it or not?'

She regarded the sickly orange dregs at the bottom of her glass with fascination. It was a damn sight easier than meeting his eyes.

'I haven't decided.'

'Which is why you're not drinking alcohol.'

'There's always adoption.'

'True.' He regarded her steadily. 'Does the father know?'

'The father's not … on the scene anymore.'

'I see.' He mused for a moment, his level gaze still on her face. 'Then I can see your dilemma. Could you give up your child after carrying it for nine months, though? I don't want to upset you, but that sounds … painful.'

Emma opened her mouth fully intending to say, 'Yes, of course I could,' but found she could not get the words out. Instead what came out was, 'Oh God,' and then she put down the glass so hard on the table next to them that it cracked, and burst into tears.

A few seconds later, Matthew was beside her, an arm round her shoulder. 'Hey,' he said gently, 'it's okay. I'm not judging you. Nobody's got the right to do that. It's your baby, your choice.'

She reached blindly into her coat pocket for a hanky, trying to control her sobs. He pressed a clean tissue into her hand. 'Th...thanks,' she managed to say.

'You're welcome.'

She dried her eyes, keeping her head bent. Crying – and in public too. She could not remember being so embarrassed for years. 'Is everyone staring?'

He paused, looking round the busy pub.

'Yes.'

'Your dad too? And Fiona – I mean, Fifi.'

'Yes.'

'Oh hell.'

'Who cares? Who gives a damn what anyone else thinks?' His arm slipped to her waist, and he hugged her close. 'I certainly don't. And you shouldn't either. Go on, let it all out.'

She dabbed her eyes. 'I think it's all out now.'

'Sure? Because I've got plenty more tissues where that one came from. And most of them are clean.'

She giggled, and pushed him away. 'I'm fine, honestly.' She crumpled up the damp tissue and pushed it into her fruit juice glass. 'God, I hate blubbing.'

'Perfectly understandable though.'

'Because of my hormones, you mean?' she asked, instantly prickly again, and hissed under her breath, 'Crazy pregnant lady hormones?'

'No, because of the all the stress you must be under,' he said mildly. 'Though I don't mind crazy pregnant ladies.'

'I told you to stop using the P word.'

'You used it first,' he pointed out.

'Don't quibble.'

'Okay,' he agreed, and smiled at her in a dazzling way. 'So, about this father.'

'Who?'

'The guy who isn't on the scene anymore,' he reminded her, 'the father of your child … Does he know about the baby?'

'That's none of your business.'

Matthew stroked his chin, then made a scrunched-up face at her. As if to say, 'Really? That's your answer?'

She struggled for a moment, then admitted, 'No, he doesn't know.'

'Doesn't he have a right to know?'

'Yes, absolutely.'

'So why haven't you told him?' He looked at her, clearly puzzled by her silence. 'Are you worried how this guy might react? Do you need someone to be there with you when you tell him, maybe? Because I'd be happy to –'

'I don't know who he is,' she burst out.

His eyes widened. 'Sorry?'

Emma folded her arms protectively over her chest, feeling very off-balance. The story of her wild, one-night-stand in Ibiza did her no credit whatsoever, and would probably make him think she was recklessly promiscuous. She still remembered her mum's acidic response. Not an experience she wanted to repeat. 'It's a long story.'

'I like long stories. I watched JFK three times.'

'It's a really, really *long* story,' Emma said.

Matthew leant back against an adjacent fruit machine. 'I've got nowhere I have to go,' he said, and gestured her to begin.

'Lupus?'

Jack sounded confused.

Their curries and rice dishes were being served, so Crystal stayed silent until the waiter had gone away again, wishing them a good dinner, before she continued with her explanation.

'Lupus, yes.' She nodded. 'It's getting better known as a condition. But there are still too few doctors who can spot it, and the tests are complicated. I was unlucky. I kept getting all these issues, and being taken into hospital. But it still took them three months to diagnose lupus.' She swallowed, remembering that awful day when she got the news. 'By that time, my liver had almost packed up.'

'And if you don't get a transplant, you'll die?'

'Wow, blunt.'

'I thought you'd prefer it.'

'I guess I do.' She tried to sound off-hand. 'But that's about it, yes. No transplant, no chance of long-term survival.'

'How long-term?'

'Anything from a few more weeks to less than a year. It's hard to be sure how long I'll last. Even the experts can't give me a figure. It all depends on whether I develop any further complications.'

'Complications?'

'That's what all the pills are for. To control my symptoms and hopefully stop my body falling apart before they can find me a donor match.'

Jack leant back in his seat, not saying anything for a moment. His face was pale, his blue eyes intent on her face. Then he said, 'You poor soul.'

Her eyes welled up with tears instantly, and she bent her head.

'Don't.'

'I can't imagine what you've been going through.'

'Please, don't.' The tears began to spill over, and she wiped one hurriedly away before it could roll down her cheek. 'I'm used to it now. I've accepted it.'

'Who could ever accept that? It's a death sentence.'

Crystal grabbed up a napkin and rubbed her wet face. She could taste salt tears in her mouth. Her make-up would be ruined. But who cared? Who cared, really?

'It's just the way things are. Nothing to be done.'

'Ah, the Blitz spirit.'

'You make it sound like an episode of *EastEnders*.'

'How close are you?' Jack raised his eyebrows when she frowned at him. 'To the top of the transplant list?'

'Close enough. But there are others in a worse state. Mothers with kids, you know. They … they need to live more than I do.'

'For God's sake,' he exploded.

'No, it's true. And I'd rather it was like that. I don't want some kid to be orphaned just so I can live.'

He studied her, sombre. 'I only met you recently, Crystal. But I don't want you to die. The more I know you, the more I want you to live. Though for purely selfish reasons, I'm afraid.'

She looked at him, unsure.

'I want a chance to get to know you better.'

'Thank you,' she said huskily.

'Much better.'

Their eyes met. Her tears began to dry and her heart sped up. Did he mean what she thought he meant?

'Is that a possibility?' he asked delicately, toying with his cutlery again. He nodded to her curry, which smelt gorgeous. 'Eat up.'

Obediently, though only because it gave her nervous hands something to do, and her gaze somewhere to look that wasn't his face, Crystal scooped some mild chicken Korma into her mouth. It was delicious. Fragrant and creamily rich at the same time.

'Good?'

'Mmm,' she managed, nodding, then swallowed. 'Is what a possibility?'

'You and me,' he said, then smiled at her confusion. 'Going to bed together. Physical intimacy. Sex.'

She was gaping at him like a goldfish.

'You've thought about it, haven't you?' he asked, still smiling.

She shut her mouth tight. Her cheeks flared with heat.

God, yes.

'No need to say anything, I can see the answer in your face. But don't worry, I've done nothing but think about it since we met. You're not alone.' His smile turned serious again. 'And I don't intend you to be alone. Not any more.'

'But you understand that –'

'That you're in trouble, yes. That you have a life-threatening condition and need a liver transplant yesterday. That you may not survive.' He nodded. 'I understand.'

She put down her fork. 'Why?'

'Because my instinct tells me you're the one,' he said simply. 'So, regardless of your current situation, I still want to pursue you.'

'*Pursue* me?'

It sounded like he was planning to hunt her down. Almost like she was an endangered species, she thought, unsure whether to be flattered or frightened.

'That's right.' Jack drank some of his lager, looking at her across the top of the glass. 'Which shouldn't be too much of a challenge, given your inability to run very fast.'

'And when you catch me?'

His eyes locked with hers. It was like drowning in honey. 'Oh, then ... Then ...'

And he lowered his voice, while Crystal listened to his promises, and held her breath hard, and let herself hope at last.

CHAPTER ELEVEN

Confession might be good for the soul, Emma thought. But it was not good for a pregnant woman's delicate stomach. She was violently unwell the day after telling Matthew everything about her reckless stupidity in Ibiza, and had to call in sick at work. Then, after rallying for a while that evening, she woke in a terrible state the following morning and again had to ring Harold with an excuse.

'Upset tummy,' Emma told him down the phone, sitting on the floor next to the toilet. She crossed her fingers. 'Probably ate something dodgy. Sorry.'

'Doctor's note?'

'Have a heart. I haven't been well enough to get round to the surgery.'

'Perfectly understandable. Except that's the second bout of suspected food poisoning you've had this month,' Harold commented, then paused. 'And you had a severe migraine attack recently. That merited two whole days off, including the writers' club meeting, which meant I had to give up my evening off to cover for you. I had cinema tickets.'

'Yes, I'm really sorry about that.'

He sighed in an exaggerated fashion. 'What are we going to do with you, Emma?'

Emma made a face at her mobile but did not bother saying anything in reply. What could she say to a comment like that, after all? String me up from the yard-arm? Batter me senseless with a copy of *War and Peace*?

'Better do whatever you need to get well as soon as possible. And next time it happens, make sure you get a doctor's note.' Harold lowered his voice confidentially. 'Sue's on the war path. Apparently, management have been cracking down on absenteeism, and she's determined to do her bit.'

She closed her eyes. 'Right, point taken.'

It was tempting to say, 'Look, I'm pregnant,' and hope that covered her for days lost due to morning sickness. But she did not want her colleagues to know about her pregnancy until she had absolutely decided what to do about it – especially if it turned out they never needed to know. That would be too awful.

Besides, she had a feeling they would soon manufacture a way to get rid of her once they knew she was expecting. That had happened to Kirsty only last year. One minute she was cheerfully telling everyone at the library that she was pregnant, and booking her maternity leave dates; the next, she had been 'let go' for reasons undisclosed, though according to Harold she had turned up late once too often. It was tempting to suspect they had given Kirsty the shove to avoid having to bring in someone new just to cover her maternity leave. But of course that would be discrimination, so another excuse had been found.

After he'd rung off, she threw her mobile across the room. Luckily the bedsit was so small it bounced harmlessly off the bed.

A buzz announced the arrival of a text.

'Bloody hell.'

Emma crawled over to the phone and turned it over. It was a message from Crystal.

You up for a few hours on the beach today or tomorrow? Best place for a chat without anyone earwigging. When do you finish work?

It was tempting to go during work hours, once she was well enough to move about the place without her stomach heaving. But if she was spotted, she would get the sack for sure. No point pushing it.

She lay on her back until her head was no longer whirling, then texted back, *How about 4pm tomorrow?*

No problem. Bring your swimsuit.

Oh God.

Emma was fifteen minutes late for work at the library the next morning. Not exactly epic lateness. But it had become a frequent occurrence over the past few weeks, thanks to her morning sickness. It seemed pregnancy was no respecter of work schedules. No doubt that was why Harold hurried out of his alcove cubby hole as she arrived, trying to flag her down.

Pretending not to see him, she dashed through the door into the inner library, already shrugging out of her jacket on her way to her computer station.

'Hang on, I need a word,' he called after her.

Emma glanced at him, harassed. 'I'm running a bit late, Harold.'

'That's what I want a word about.'

She frowned, and turned around, walking quickly back towards him. She was uncomfortably aware that her tummy was still dodgy. She had not eaten anything for breakfast, her only concession to hunger being a cup of mild ginger tea, supposed to calm queasiness, but that had not helped as much as she had hoped.

'I'm sorry I'm in late, I missed the bus,' she told him, lying and feeling bad about it. But she could hardly admit that it had been one hell of a job to drag herself out of bed this morning, and he was lucky she was here at all. 'I ran all the way.'

'I can see you're out of breath.' Harold sighed, then ran a hand through his untidy hair. 'Problem is, you're out of luck too.'

'What do you mean?'

He jerked his head towards the upper floor. 'Sue wants to see you.'

Sue was their boss.

She knew what that meant. 'Oh shh …'

'Emma!'

Harold indicated a heavily pregnant mother waddling past with her toddler in search of the toilets; the woman glanced at them wide-eyed before hurrying on, protectively covering her child's ears.

'Shine a light,' Emma finished awkwardly.

'Look, it's probably nothing serious. But she did want to see your record, and asked about any instances of late arrival, late returns from lunch, that kind of thing.'

'So what did you tell her?'

Harold looked nonplussed. 'The truth, of course.'

'Thanks.'

'Emma, I want to help you. But there's no point trying to pull the wool over anyone's eyes in management. The council has all that on computer anyway. Sue was just asking me for –'

'Your opinion on whether she should fire me or not?'

'Confirmation of the data she's already got in hand, actually.' Harold looked at her pityingly. 'I don't want it to sound like I'm saying, I told you so. But I told you so. You keep rolling in late like this, and taking days off without a doctor's note or any proper explanation, the powers-that-be are going to come down hard on you.'

'I've been ill.'

'I know, I told her that. I did my best to cover for you. I said, Emma's not herself, she's been ill, yada yada yada.' Harold shrugged, a gesture of helplessness. 'I don't think Sue was interested. No doctor's note, see?'

She closed her eyes. Bloody hell.

'Love, you don't look too wonderful today,' her mum said, gazing through the door at Crystal with very little evidence of maternal concern. She noted the baskets of white linen, most still soiled, and her brow creased even more. 'I suppose you need me to do the washing today, after all.'

'No, I can manage.'

Crystal had offered to do the main linen wash that week. They sent the bed sheets out to a laundry service, but there were still the napkins and tablecloths. Those they tended to wash and dry themselves in the small utility room to save on laundry costs, which were already exorbitant. But it was true that she had underestimated how tired she would feel, shovelling armfuls of hot linen in and out of the two large machines in a steamy atmosphere.

'You don't look like you can manage.'

'Please, mum …'

She wiped her forehead, a little unsteady, unable to finish her sentence. But she was annoyed. Her thoughts about Jack were steamy enough without adding the reality of laundry to them.

'Perhaps you should come and sit down in the kitchen,' Fiona suggested helpfully. 'Take five. I could make tea.'

'Out,' Crystal said, pointing to the door. 'I said I would do it. So I'm going to do it. Just leave me to … do it.'

Her mother grumbled, shaking her head. 'Suit yourself. Only don't blame me if you end up back in hospital for another six weeks, surrounded by flowers and grapes.'

'Stop exaggerating.'

'I'll have to take out shares in Interflora at this rate.'

'What part of "stop exaggerating" didn't you understand?'

'I'm going, I'm going,' Fiona said, and waved her hand dismissively. 'Go ahead, knock yourself out.'

Which wasn't far from the truth.

As soon as the door had closed behind her mother, Crystal slid down the steam-damp wall and collapsed on the floor of the utility room. Her legs were trembling. And she felt sick again. Sick and dizzy.

She was determined not to let this bloody thing beat her though. Not to let lupus dictate what she could or couldn't do. Her mum had been right. She only had one life. And she intended to make the most of it.

After five minutes of slow breathing with her eyes closed, Crystal felt recovered enough to stand up and continue work. For all of thirty seconds, that was, before her body rebelled again.

Her legs wobbled.

Her whole body felt like it was made of lead.

Her head was pounding.

But she held onto the tumble drier for support, and bit her lip.

Damn bloody lupus.

This afternoon she was going to the bloody beach with her bloody new friend Emma and they would have a bloody good time together.

Even if it killed her.

The lift doors opened, and her supervisor Sue pranced out on three-inch black patent heels. Emma took one look at her face, and her heart sank. Sue was looking officious and a bit smug in a grey blouse with a big bow at the neck, a sheaf of manila folders clutched to her chest.

Bad news, in other words. And Sue was enjoying it.

'Ah, Emma, there you are at last.' Her supervisor stopped right in front of her, eyes wide with feigned innocence and friendliness. Not to mention lashes dripping with thick black mascara. 'What a pleasant surprise. I was beginning to wonder if you would turn into work at all today.'

The tone of withering sarcasm was not lost on Emma. Or on Harold, to judge by his uncomfortable expression.

'I'm really sorry I'm late, Sue. I can explain what happened.

'Of course you can. There's always a reason. Nobody is ever late for work *deliberately*. Especially not day after day.' Sue smiled blandly at her before shepherding her back towards the lift. 'Shall we go upstairs for a chat?'

Emma said nothing. But she was thinking, *do I have a choice? Because if so, no thanks.*

'I'll hold the fort down here, shall I?' Harold asked Sue, looking nervous as the lift doors began to close.

Sue studied him without saying anything, her narrow brows slightly raised. It was clear she did not think much of Harold either. Probably because he liked Emma.

I'd better warn him about that, Emma thought wearily, and averted her gaze from Harold's face. Being seen to be too friendly to a disgraced colleague like her could prove the kiss of death to his own career. She had not always got along with Harold. He was a pleasant guy, as qualified librarians go, but he could be every bit as officious and penny-pinching as Sue at times. That did not mean she wanted the poor man dragged down with her though.

The lift doors shut with a dull metallic clang, and the whole box gave an awful shudder. The lift was ancient, like the rest of the library buildings. It was constantly out of order or under repair. Ideally, it needed to be replaced. But of course there was no money for anything new these days. Not even books.

Which was ironic, given that it was a library.

Sue glanced at her watch. 'You're supposed to start at nine, aren't you? I make it nearly half past now.'

'I missed the bus,' Emma said, feeling sick again.

The lift lurched into motion, dragging itself up to the third floor like a wounded animal. The noise it made was quite horrendous too.

Sue was wearing very strong perfume. Strong and cheap. Her shiny grey blouse must be drenched in it. Or was that just an olfactory hallucination?

'You miss the bus rather frequently.'

'I'm sorry.'

Sue's smile was chilly. 'Punctuality, Emma. Reliability. It's the one thing that makes a team member really valuable.'

'Those are two things.'

'Sorry?'

'You said, punctuality and reliability are the one thing that …'

'Don't quibble, it makes you sound petty.' Sue waved her thick manila folders at her. 'Paperwork, computers, administration. Those are the buzzwords these days, in terms of employability. Not getting the adjective right.'

'They're nouns.'

'What are?'

'Punctuality and reliability.'

'I know that,' Sue said angrily. 'I have a PhD, thank you very much. It was just a figure of speech.'

The lift juddered to a halt on the third floor. Emma held onto the wall to support herself. She felt dizzy and very, very unwell.

The doors began to open.

'Oh, come on,' Sue exclaimed, glaring at her. 'There's no use pretending to be ill. I'm not falling for that old chestnut.'

Emma tried to speak, but the words would not come out. She swallowed hard, trying to control her sickness.

'Now listen, Emma. I know we're council-run here, and things aren't as strict as they would be in private enterprise. But you've had as much leeway from the management team as you're going to get. So it's time you and I had a serious chat about your future with this library.' Sue's perfume was almost overpowering in the small space. 'And amateur dramatics will do you no good at all.'

That perfume. It was like chemical warfare.

Emma's stomach suddenly rebelled.

She tried in vain to push Sue away. For her own protection. 'Please …'

'Don't you shove me,' Sue began indignantly, refusing

to budge, but it was too late. She gave an ear-piercing shriek as Emma groaned and threw up over her feet. 'Oh my God. What the hell?'

'Sorry,' Emma mumbled.

Sue didn't say anything else. She didn't need to. Emma knew what her boss was thinking as she stared down at her ruined tights and heels.

She was so bloody fired.

CHAPTER TWELVE

Emma and Crystal met up in the car park near the beach, and walked down together in the afternoon sunshine. The beach café was still open and doing a brisk trade by the look of it, a dozen or so people eating outside at the open air tables that faced the ocean.

Emma gave a quick glance through the café door as they passed, but did not stop.

Crystal grinned at her. 'Hankering after an ice cream?'

Emma's answering smile was a little uncertain. 'Maybe later.' She looked her up and down. 'Jeans? On the beach?'

Crystal felt too awkward to admit the truth, which was that her legs had been horribly blotchy by the time she went upstairs to get changed for the beach. The last thing she wanted was to have people staring at her. Though she knew she would have to take off her jeans eventually if she wanted to swim. But perhaps by then the swelling and unsightly redness might have subsided. Her symptoms often disappeared as quickly as they flared up, leaving her with nothing to show by the time she reached the local surgery or the casualty department at hospital.

At least, she was keeping her fingers crossed that her symptoms would have disappeared. If not, she might have to give up the idea of a cool, refreshing dip in the Atlantic Ocean.

'My legs are so pasty, I didn't feel like wearing shorts today,' she lied. 'Don't worry though, I'm still up for a swim. I've got my swimming cossie on underneath.'

'Excellent, so have I.'

Crystal admired her friend's summer dress, which hugged her generous chest before flaring out at the hips and falling swishily to her knees. Very stylish, especially with its pattern of luscious red cherries repeated on a cream background. It wasn't obvious that Emma was expecting a baby, she thought. But it was early days yet, of course.

'Lovely dress.'

'Thanks.'

They reached the end of the beach front, and stood looking out at the sands and the rolling sea beyond.

'Whereabouts should we sit, do you think?' Crystal gestured to her capacious beach bag. It was her mum's capacious beach bag, in fact, which she had borrowed for this special occasion. 'I brought two roll-up mats and two towels, just in case you'd forgotten. For sitting on. Sometimes the sand gets a little damp here.'

Emma grinned. 'I brought towels too. But don't worry, I'm sure we'll find a use for all of them. Some for sitting on, some for drying off.'

'I brought a few colouring books too. And some pens.'

'What a good idea.'

'So where would you like to set up camp?'

'How about over there? Under the rocks.'

Crystal eyed the area she was pointing at, well past the rocky foreshore. The sand looked fairly dry, and it was equidistant between the incoming tide and the beach café. 'Looks like a great sun trap. Come on.' She set off down the steps onto the beach, though her legs were still killing her. 'We can have a sunbathe first while we chat, then a quick swim, then maybe an ice cream.'

'Perfect.' Emma laughed. 'We could be sisters.'

'How's that?'

'Because you took the words right out of my mouth. Like you could read my mind.'

Crystal was flattered. She balanced painfully over the large white and grey pebbles on their way to the sandy area, and tried not to wince.

'I often wish I'd had a sister.'

'Me too, me too. Are you an only child as well?'

'I'm afraid so.'

Emma grimaced. 'Then you'll understand. People always assume you've had an easy life as an only child. That you must be spoilt, a total brat. The one who got all the toys. But it's nothing like that, is it?'

'No, you get all the baggage instead.'

'Absolutely.'

'All the parental angst, all the pressure to succeed.'

'Tell me about it.'

'Nothing's ever good enough for them.'

'Sounds like you and I could be cosmic twins.'

'And they never let go.'

Emma paused, still looking amused by the conversation. But Crystal caught a sudden flicker of pain behind her smile. A raw nerve had been touched, she guessed. 'Parents, huh?'

'Still, what can you do? They're your parents, right?' Crystal stopped walking. 'What do you think, is this the right spot?'

They both looked round at the sandy spot near the base of the cliffs. It was dryish and sunny, and it should take the incoming tide at least an hour to reach them in that position, Crystal guessed. Maybe slightly less. But long enough for a chat and a dip in the foaming shallows before they had to retreat back up to the café for an ice cream.

'Looks perfect to me.'

Crystal nodded her agreement, set down her bag, and began to unroll the silvery beach mats.

'I'm so glad we did this,' Emma said.

'Me too.'

They unpacked their gear and chose a flat spot for the beach mats, both facing the sea as though they planned to worship it. The sea breeze whipped at their hair occasionally, but the afternoon warmth was still very pleasant. Once they were both lying on the mats – now covered with beach towels, and weighed down with large stones at each corner – and the sun was baking down on their prone bodies, Crystal glanced at Emma's pensive face and decided to come clean about her own little secret.

She had been putting off the awful moment too long as it was. It was time to 'fess up.

'You know what you told me about Ibiza?'

Emma sounded guarded. 'Yes.'

'Well, as long as you promise not to say a word to anyone, I've got my own confession to make.'

'You're not pregnant too, are you?'

Crystal rolled her eyes. 'God, if only it were that simple.'

'You think being pregnant is simple? Especially on my own?'

'Sorry, of course not. That came out all wrong. I just meant … Oh, it doesn't matter.' Crystal bit her lip, leaning up on her elbow to look at her new friend. 'I shouldn't have said anything, forget it.'

'But you did.'

'I know, sorry, sorry.'

'Crystal, quit stalling and tell me your confession. I'm listening.'

'Okay, I'm not very well,' she announced abruptly.

Emma sat up too, shielding her eyes against the glare of the sun to gaze at Crystal. She had an odd expression on her face, as though she had expected to hear something different.

'Oh dear. Do you need to go home?'

Crystal realised she had not explained herself very well.

'No, I'm fine right now. More or less. I meant I've got a long term illness.'

Emma studied her. 'How horrid for you. Nothing serious, I hope?'

Crystal sighed. Everyone always said that.

'It is quite serious, unfortunately. I've got a condition called lupus.'

'Lupus?' Emma's eyes widened, fixed on her face. 'I've heard of that. It can affect your immune system, can't it?'

Crystal was surprised. 'Among other things. But essentially, yes. Well done. Most people have no idea what it is.'

'I've only heard of lupus because I watch so many medical shows on the telly. It's the condition patients always have on that show *House*. You know, whenever Dr House and his team can't work out what's wrong with a patient, it usually turns out to be lupus.' Emma narrowed her eyes. 'Probably because it has so many different symptoms.'

'That's right.'

'Gosh, are you okay? I mean, are you feeling ill right now? Do I need to do anything? Call someone?'

Crystal grinned. 'No, I'm good. Well, my legs are hurting today. For no reason I can think of. Another of my wonderful mystery symptoms that spring up overnight.'

'Mystery?'

'I call them that because the doctors never know why they happen. Like my arm might suddenly swell up, or my skin start tingling for no apparent reason. Once I woke up and my ear was bleeding … from the inside.'

Emma stared at her in horror. 'Ugh.'

'Sorry.' Crystal bit her lip, instantly contrite. 'I didn't mean to come across all gruesome. I'm so used to icky stuff like that now, it no longer affects me the same way. When I was first diagnosed, I was forever in and out of hospital, thinking I was at death's door. But they'd just give me more pills, and the swelling would go down or the bleeding would stop.'

She looked out to sea. If only it was as simple as that. But she did not want to alarm her new friend too much and drive her away.

'Now it takes a major incident for me even to mention it to the doctor. Like, maybe if my leg fell off I might give the hospital a quick call.'

It was a joke. Emma didn't laugh though.

'But isn't that dangerous? What if it turns out to be something really serious?'

'I have to live my life, Emma. I can't always assume I'm about to die. Even when ... even when it feels like I am.'

'You poor thing.'

Crystal felt her eyes tear up. 'Don't, please.' She reached into her bag for her sunglasses and put them on, embarrassed by her own reaction. 'Don't pity me. Laugh at me. Or with me, at least. I prefer that. I know it's a serious condition. I know I could die. But I'd rather put that knowledge to one side and just enjoy my life as much as possible.'

Emma pulled her knees close to her chin, watching her. The sea breeze whipped a little sand around them, the noise of the waves louder now. 'Could you though?'

'Could I what?'

'Die.'

'Pretty much, yes.'

Emma frowned. 'I thought there was a treatment for lupus.'

'There is. But by the time they'd worked out what was wrong with me, I'd had all these other speculative treatments, and my liver was shot to pieces. So yes, I could die. If I don't get a transplant soon.'

'I'll donate.'

Crystal was shocked. 'What?'

'I'll donate some of my liver. People can do that, can't they?'

'Oh my God, you're serious.' Crystal shook her head.

'Just like that. You'd risk your own life to save a stranger's?'

Emma made a face. 'You're not a stranger. We're friends now, aren't we? Besides, if it means helping you survive …'

'You'd have to be a match. And you couldn't have any health problems yourself. You'd have to be one hundred and ten percent fit.'

'Well, I am,' Emma said swiftly. Her face grew pale. 'Although … I suppose …'

'You're having a baby.'

'Shit.'

'Look, don't worry about it.' Crystal felt awful. She should never have mentioned the lupus in the first place. In fact, she had only done so because she did not want there to be any secrets between them. 'Honestly, it's fine. It's all under control. I'm on a national transplant list. As soon as I reach the top of the list, and a suitable match becomes available, the hospital will call me in for surgery. Simple as that.'

'Right,' Emma said slowly.

'What you offered me though … It was very generous of you. Too kind, really.' Crystal reached out and squeezed Emma's hand. 'Please don't feel bad. I wanted you to know, that's all.'

'Of course. Thank you for telling me.'

'I didn't want to rush off sick one day, and have you think I didn't like you. Or was bloody rude. Or whatever.'

Emma's eyes were swimming with tears. 'I would never think that.'

Oh God, she'd made her friend cry.

'I'm sorry.'

'No, I'm sorry,' Emma insisted, and wiped away a tear. 'My fault. I shouldn't have been so crass. Speaking without my brain in gear.'

'Now I've made you blub.'

'No, no, honestly.' But Emma snatched her hand back,

and buried her face between her drawn-up knees. She was crying. 'I meant it, you know. I really wanted to help you. I'd forgotten about the baby.'

Horrified, Crystal struggled up onto her knees, though they felt badly swollen, and gave Emma a hug. It was hard not to yelp with pain. What the hell was up with her legs today?

'Please don't cry. Honestly, it's okay.'

'I'm not crying because of that … I'm crying because …' She added something unintelligible.

'Sorry?'

'Because I'm lost.' Emma looked up at her, her eyes red-rimmed, cheeks damp with tears. 'I don't know what to do.'

'About the baby?'

'I can't keep it, Crystal. I want to, but I just can't.'

'Okay.'

'My parents don't want to help out. I don't know who the father is. I've got no money, no savings to speak of. I'm living in this awful, tiny bedsit … and now … now I've lost my job.'

'You've lost your job? At the library?'

'I should have seen it coming. I kept taking time off without a doctor's note. I was constantly late for work. Then I threw up over my boss. Not my finest hour.'

'I'm so sorry.'

'That's why I can't possibly have this baby. You understand?'

'Yes.'

'It's out of the question.'

'Okay.'

'How can you say that?' Emma asked. 'How can you say "okay" like it means nothing? This is my baby we're talking about.'

'Okay.'

'Oh God, Crystal. What am I going to do?'

Crystal looked at the sea, at how the inevitable rush of

the tide was encroaching on the beach, and thought hard. She had no idea what it would feel like to be pregnant and alone, but tried to put herself in Emma's shoes. Though her friend's feet were bare and covered with a fine dusting of sand. Same difference, as her mum would say. What would she do if she were pregnant under the same circumstances as Emma? Apart from panic and run about screaming, she told herself. That kind of advice would be unhelpful right now. Albeit honest.

It was not like her own life was particularly easy, after all. She ought to be able to help Emma, even if she could not help herself.

'First,' she said slowly, 'I'd look for somewhere else to live. Somewhere that was better suited to a single mum, and where being late with the rent wouldn't be such a big deal. You're sure you can't go home?'

Emma shook her head.

'Well, why not come and live with us then? You could share my room at first, if that doesn't sound too awful. Just until you're sorted out with benefits or another job. We have plenty of space, and I wouldn't mind a room-mate.'

Emma dried her eyes, looking perplexed. 'Live with you?'

'Why not?'

'But your mother –'

'I'm sure Mum wouldn't say no,' Crystal said promptly, though she was crossing her fingers behind her back. 'She's quite easy-going. And if you were able to help out round the place, that would be brilliant. I'm a bit useless at the moment, what with having funny spells every other day. So she's run off her feet with all the laundry and cleaning and doing the breakfasts. Especially when we're at full capacity, as we usually are during the season.'

'That's so generous.'

'I want to help.' Crystal shrugged. 'And it does sound like you're in a fix, what with your bedsit and losing your job. But if you move in with us, that would give you options. Not to mention a breathing space while you decide what to do for the best.'

Emma nodded, though she was still looking uncertain. 'I'll have to ask your mum.'

'No problem.' Crystal grinned, sitting back with a quick grimace. God, her legs were hurting so badly. The pain was becoming insane; it was like having hundreds of tiny pins pushed deep into her thighs and the backs of her knees. All the same, she felt happier than when they'd arrived at the beach. She could not do very much for herself, but it was good to know she'd made some difference to Emma's mood, at least. 'So, colouring books or swim?'

Emma laughed. 'Swim, I think. If you're up to that.'

'Definitely.' With difficulty, Crystal pushed herself to her feet, wincing at the discomfort. 'My legs are boiling in these jeans. I can't wait to get into the water, cool myself down.'

But when she undid her jeans, and tried to push them down, she found it hard to get them beyond mid-thigh. 'Oh, bloody hell.'

'What is it?'

'Erm, nothing.' Embarrassed, Crystal turned away and tried again. But it was hopeless. Her legs were so swollen and blotchy, she couldn't actually remove her jeans. 'For God's sake.'

Emma had already whipped off her dress and was standing on the towel in her one-piece swimsuit, looking a little nervous.

It was not obvious that she was pregnant, Crystal thought, unable to stop herself sneaking a little peek at her friend's tummy. But though Emma's lower abdomen was not so rounded, it was not entirely flat either. Early days, she supposed. She could imagine it would feel odd though, knowing there was a tiny life in there, starting to take root.

'Can I help?'

'What, take my jeans off for me? Like I'm a kid?'

'Sorry.'

They looked at each other for a minute. Then Crystal burst out laughing, and Emma laughed too, a little ruefully.

'This is crazy.'

Emma bit her lip as though to stop herself giggling. 'It is a bit. But let's approach this logically. What exactly is the problem?'

'The problem is, I seem to have got fatter on the way to the beach. So fat I can't actually get my jeans down my legs.'

'That's impossible.'

'Seriously, they're not going anywhere.' Crystal tugged at her jeans crossly. 'And it hurts.'

'Now, that's *not* funny.' Emma frowned as she studied her. 'I know it's undignified, but perhaps you should sit down and let me try tugging them off you.'

'Bum on the towel, legs in the air?'

'Sounds right.'

Crystal rolled her eyes. 'I guess it's the only way I'm going to get a dip today. And to tell you the truth, I'm desperate to lose these jeans now.' She lowered herself gingerly onto the towel and held up her legs, making a face. 'My legs feel like they're on fire.'

Glancing at her red-raw thighs, Emma looked horrified. 'God, I'm not surprised. Are you sure you don't need a doctor?'

'One step at a time. Or leg, in this case. Honestly, they may look better after I've been swimming. These things flare up and disappear so quickly.' Crystal nodded as Emma took hold of both hems at the same time. 'Right, just go for it.'

'On three?'

She took a deep breath, then let it go, counting aloud with Emma. 'One … two … three.'

Emma dragged violently on her jeans and they shifted down to her swollen knees, then off. Crystal shrieked as a wave of the most exquisite pain rippled up her spine.

'I'm sorry, I'm sorry,' Emma gabbled, backing away with the jeans in her hands.

Crystal swore long and loud, shaking uncontrollably. 'No ... problem,' she managed to say, though now they were exposed to the air, her legs felt as though someone had rubbed broken glass up and down her skin. 'Th ... thanks.'

But Emma was still staring. 'Oh my God.'

'What?'

'Your legs, your poor legs ...'

She glanced down at herself. She was wearing her bikini beneath her clothes, so was decent, but ... Then she saw how red and vast her knees were. And her calves and thighs looked like they'd been inflated by a bicycle pump. And she felt dizzy just looking at them. Sick and dizzy.

Even by her standards this was not good. Something was wrong. Badly, horrifically wrong.

'Hey, you two okay?'

They looked round to see Matthew sprinting over from the beach café, a tea towel flapping over his shoulder. Boris's son, the new guy who'd come to the colouring book club and left with Emma.

Crystal remembered seeing him down here before, clearing tables at the café for his dad. A good-looking bloke, though not her type, older by a few years, and a bit too athletic and outdoorsy for her tastes.

She spotted at once that Emma did not share her response, however. Her friend's eyes had widened, and suddenly Emma was sucking in her stomach and pressing back her shoulders, and generally looking nervous. As though the two of them were now an item, which judging by how Matthew was also looking straight at Emma's face, in that 'I'm not going to say this out loud, but God I fancy you' way, was almost certainly the truth.

'Are you okay?' he asked Emma, staring at her as though she was the one who was sick.

'I'm fine. Please don't fuss. It's her,' she said bluntly, pointing at Crystal, 'who needs help.'

He tore his gaze from Emma's face, and looked properly at Crystal. His shock was palpable as he took in the state of her bare legs, which felt utterly enormous. 'Christ, what the hell happened to you? Have you been stung?'

'Stung?'

'By a jellyfish?' Matthew was breathing hard, a red tinge in his cheeks. He was genuinely concerned for her, which was touching. 'I saw Emma pulling your jeans off, and thought ... God, that looks bad.'

Crystal suddenly realised she was still shaking. It must be some kind of massive auto-immune reaction. But to what? She tried to think what she had eaten, what she had drunk, what she had been doing for the past twenty-four hours. But there was no obvious cause. Not that there needed to be an obvious cause these days. Her body was acutely sensitive to even the tiniest stress or change in environment.

She wanted to reassure her friends. But all she could do was repeat words as though she could not comprehend language anymore.

'J ... jellyfish?'

'We haven't even been in the water yet,' Emma told him urgently.

'Was it a wasp, then? An insect bite? That's one hell of a reaction. There's an EpiPen in the First Aid kit at the café. Shall I run and fetch it?'

Crystal tried to gather her thoughts, to make sense. Her lips felt vaguely numb now, so that even speaking was becoming difficult.

'N ... no need. Not a sting. Not sure what it is. But ... I think ... I'd better go to hospital.'

Matthew did not argue, but turned at once to Emma. 'I don't suppose you have a phone?'

Emma seemed dazed. But nodded. 'Of course.' Then

she suddenly came alive, reaching for her bag. 'Sorry, yes. Hold on. My mobile's in here somewhere.' She fished the mobile out of her bag, still looking in horror at Crystal's swollen legs, then rang 999 and listened.

'Hello? We need an ambulance. Yes, it's an emergency.'

CHAPTER THIRTEEN

The helicopter came for Crystal, not an ambulance, as speed was important. It landed in the tennis courts near the beach, rotor blades whirring noisily. By that time, Emma could see that Crystal was so far gone she could barely speak anymore, her face pale, her eyes closed. But Matthew had rung to let her mum know what had happened – Boris had Fiona's number up on the wall at the café, apparently – and so at least Crystal had not been whisked off to hospital on her own.

'You want to go too, don't you?' Matthew had asked, watching her face as she followed the disappearing helicopter across the sky.

So Matthew had driven Emma to Truro hospital so she could make sure Crystal was okay. But of course it was a long drive by road, and when they arrived, there was no sign of Crystal or her mum.

She joined the queue to speak to the receptionist. The emergency department was busy, as was usual in the summer season. Kids fallen off bikes or skateboards by the look of it, most of them, but there were a few frail old people too, and a couple of burly builders on the front row of seats, arms folded, looking impatiently at the clock.

'I'm here for my friend,' she told the harassed-looking receptionist, and gave Crystal's name. 'She has lupus. They brought her in by helicopter.'

The woman tapped at the keyboard, then nodded. 'She's still being treated. Through there.' She nodded towards the double doors into the treatment area. 'But if you're not family, I'm afraid you'll have to wait. I'll let you know once they're done with her. Looks like she'll be going up onto the wards afterwards.'

'But is she going to be okay?'

'I'm sorry, I can't –'

'I don't want to make a nuisance of myself,' Emma said, making a total nuisance of herself. 'But I can't just sit here, not knowing how she is or what's going on back there. She's my friend. We were together when … when she was taken ill.'

The receptionist looked at her, unblinking. 'I don't have any answers for you.'

'I'm not going away until I know. I physically can't. Just tell me if my friend's okay.' Emma was pleading with the woman now. 'Please.'

There was an other woman in the reception area, busy with filing. She glanced round at Emma's face, and bent over the receptionist, saying, 'Let me have a quick word with Penny. See if I can't find something out for this lady.'

Emma smiled at her over the receptionist's head. 'Oh, thank you. That's very kind.'

'Wait here.'

She stood to one side while the woman disappeared through the doors into the treatment area. The receptionist glared at her, then raised her eyebrows at the man behind Emma.

'Next?'

After a few more minutes of agonising impatience, the woman returned, her air brisk, her smile deliberately unrevealing. 'Your friend will be a little while yet. They're doing tests. But she's stable now. So that's good news.'

'Thank you.'

A little more relieved now she knew Crystal was not at death's door, Emma slipped back through the busy casualty department. Matthew was leaning against the wall by the entrance doors, a worried frown on his face.

He straightened as she approached. 'How is she?'

'Still undergoing tests, they said.'

'For?'

'They won't tell me anything else except that she's stable. I'll have to hang around a while longer if I want to see her.' She thought for a moment. 'Look, it was very kind of you to run me here. But this could take ages. You should go. I'll get the bus home.'

'Not a chance.'

Emma smiled at him. He really was very sweet. Even with his dishevelled fair hair that had flopped over one eye.

'If you're sure …'

'Of course I'm sure.' Matthew studied her, still frowning. 'You're really quite pale, you know that? You look done in.'

'Probably the baby.'

'No, it's all this worry over Crystal.'

He was not wrong there, she thought wearily.

'Right.' As though sensing her sudden lack of direction, Matthew took her arm in a firm grip. 'Come on, I spotted a café opposite the car park. Let's grab a coffee while we wait for news.'

With anyone else, she might have been offended by his bossy manner. But right now, she needed someone to take charge. She had been thrown by Crystal's unexpected and dramatic collapse, despite knowing about her friend's illness. Adrenalin had flooded her system back at the beach, allowing her to stay calm and respond quickly. But now that everything was under control, and Crystal was undergoing treatment, that surge of adrenalin was draining away. And with it, she was losing energy fast.

'Good idea.'

She felt herself stumble as they headed back towards the main hospital buildings, and made a face at her own stupidity. The world was spinning slightly. Low blood sugar?

'Perhaps I should eat something, actually,' Emma mumbled, hanging onto his arm for support. 'I didn't have breakfast. Or lunch, in fact. Now I feel … rather …'

'Oh, no,' he said sharply. 'Not you too.'

Matthew caught her in his arms. Before she knew what was happening, he had hoisted her against his chest and begun to half-drag, half-carry her back towards the Accident and Emergency Department.

Emma tried to stay upright but her legs felt like jelly, and it was all she could do to stay conscious. She was frightened now, wondering what on earth could be wrong with her. 'What the …'

His voice in her ear was reassuring. 'Hush, don't try to talk. Nearly there.'

A nurse was fussing round her now. People were staring. The receptionist with the sharp voice was asking Matthew for her personal details. The doors into the treatment area banged open, and next thing Emma knew, she was being helped onto a high bed surrounded by curtains.

'She's pregnant,' Matthew was saying helpfully.

'How far along?'

'I'm not sure. A few months?'

One nurse was taking her pulse. Another was arranging the pillows under her head, her movements brisk and impersonal. 'Hello, Emma? Can you hear me?'

'Of course I can hear you.'

'Okay, a bit of sass. That's good. Shows you're on the mend. No, don't try to sit up.' The nurse pulled up the safety rail on the bed, like she was a child who might roll off and hurt herself. 'You went all wobbly on us, Emma. Best to stay still for a while.'

She felt so embarrassed. 'I'm fine, honestly. There's

nothing wrong with me. I just skipped a few meals, that's all.'

'Not a good idea when you're expecting.'

'Expecting what?'

The nurse laughed. 'I like your sense of humour.'

She looked round the small curtained cubicle. 'Where's Matthew?'

'Is that the guy you came in with? I sent him to the foyer to fetch you a nice cup of hot, sweet tea.'

'Sweet … Ugh.'

'He said you'd had a bit of a shock.' The nurse winked at her, her tone conspiratorial. 'Listen, I hate sugar in tea too. But trust me, this'll do the trick. Think of it as medicine. Down the little red hatch.'

Then the doctor came in.

Emma lay still, watching with instinctive distrust as the doctor and nurse talked quietly for a moment, turned away from her so she couldn't hear.

She hated white coats. It was a recognised phobia, apparently. Doctors, surgeons, lab technicians. Anyone with a white coat, she got the cold sweats, regardless. Her dad had laughed at her more than once because of it. But it wasn't her fault. In the presence of a white coat, she felt the same way animals did at the vet's: scared witless, and desperate to be somewhere else.

The doctor smiled at her. 'Hello, I'm Penny.'

'Oh.' Emma stared. 'You're treating my friend too, I think.'

'What's your friend's name?'

'Crystal.'

'Of course.' The doctor smiled, and turned to clean her hands at the small wall sink, rubbing in some antibacterial gel. 'No need to look so terrified. I'm going to give you a little examination, if that's okay.'

'Examination?'

'You're pregnant, I believe you said.' The doctor came towards her, an understanding smile on her face. When

Emma shrank away instinctively, she paused, the smile fading a little. 'You don't need to undress if you'd rather not.'

'Well, I'm here with a guy.'

'And you don't want him to walk in and find you lying here with everything on show, is that it?'

'You must be psychic.'

The doctor grinned at the nurse, who had come back into the room with several packs of plastic gloves. Like they were about to give her an internal.

'You may have to get used to that idea, I'm afraid. If you want him with you during labour.'

'During labour?' Emma felt heat in her cheeks. 'Oh no, I … He's not … that is …'

'Hey, just try keeping me away,' Matthew drawled from behind the curtain. He mock-knocked on the flimsy material. 'Are you decent? May I come in?'

Shocked speechless, Emma could only stare.

Matthew wanted to be there with her during the birth itself? But he wasn't the father. They barely knew each other. She kept thinking of how he had taken the news of her crazy promiscuity in Ibiza. So calmly, so without judgement. He had appeared to understand perfectly how it had happened, and did not even berate her for not making sure she took emergency protection afterwards. It had all been such a blur, she had told him, and he had nodded.

But it was one thing to understand her predicament and even sympathise, and another to want a relationship with her when she was pregnant with an unknown stranger's baby.

Besides, she still wasn't one hundred percent sure if she was keeping the baby. Or was she?

The doctor was feeling her tummy now with gentle hands, frowning slightly, her expression distracted. Not that there was much to feel. Maybe a bump the size of a small apple, just beginning to swell in that narrow space between the bones of Emma's pelvis.

'Hmm,' the doctor said under her breath, pressing harder. 'Hmm.'

Emma stared up at her. 'What?'

'Oh, nothing.'

'No, you said … *Hmm*. Like there was something to be worried about.' She tried to sit up and was pushed back into place by the doctor, whose friendly eyes looked concerned now. 'Oh my God, what is it? Is the baby alright?'

'There's absolutely nothing to be worried about,' Penny reassured her.

'But?'

'But it might be a good idea to listen to baby's heartbeat.'

Emma could hardly breathe for a minute. She looked at Matthew's face, then at the doctor. 'You can do that?'

The doctor raised her eyebrows. 'Of course, with a Sonicaid device. From the size of your tummy, I'd say you must be heading towards the end of your first trimester. Have you not had any antenatal care yet?'

Emma shook her head, suddenly perturbed. 'I was waiting for a better time. Waiting to … to be sure.'

Truth be told, she had not wanted to go to the antenatal clinic on her own. It had been too alien and disturbing a world. And her parents had not spoken to her since she'd told them about the baby.

'Then we'd better have a listen now.' She nodded to the nurse, who turned to help Emma with her dress. 'Do you want your friend to leave first?'

Matthew looked at her, saying nothing.

'Not if he wants to stay,' Emma heard herself say, much to her own surprise, and saw his slow smile.

'I'll hold your hand,' he promised her, and sat down by her head, taking her hand in his. His eyes met hers, an ironic gleam in them. 'And I won't look at anything below the waist, I swear.'

She could not help smiling too. 'Thanks,' she said huskily.

The nurse tucked up her dress, and the doctor leant forward over her tummy with a bottle of gel.

'Erm …'

'What is it?' Emma was instantly alarmed. 'What's wrong?'

The nurse and doctor both looked up at her.

'You're wearing a swimsuit,' the nurse said, her voice almost deliberately blank.

Emma blushed. 'Oh yes. We were on the beach. Sorry. Does it make a difference?

The doctor was bemused. 'Well, I can hardly squirt this on your tummy when I can't get to your tummy,' she pointed out.

Matthew got up. 'I'll stand outside the curtain while you get rid of your swimsuit,' he said calmly. 'If you want me back in after that, just call.'

A few desperate tugs, rustles and inward struggles later, and Emma was once more lying on her back, this time with a huge roll of green paper discreetly covering her important bits, with just her lower abdomen exposed.

'You can come back in now,' she called to Matthew, who drew back the curtain and joined her again with only the faintest hint of a smirk on his face.

'You're not laughing at me, are you?' she asked him suspiciously.

'Not at all.'

'Because I wouldn't like that.'

'I'm taking this very seriously,' Matthew assured her, and gave her hand a quick squeeze. 'Anyway, I would never laugh at you openly.'

She glared at him.

'Ready?' the doctor asked, smiling at them both.

Emma was not feeling ready for this. Not even

remotely. But she nodded.

The doctor warned her, 'Cold on your tummy,' as she spread a dollop of gel over her lower abdomen. 'Now let's have a listen with the Sonicaid, see if we can hear baby's heartbeat.'

Emma held her breath, looking into Matthew's eyes.

She felt the equipment being pressed quite hard into her belly. The doctor frowned, moving it slowly from side to side.

Silence.

The doctor's frown deepened. She glanced at the nurse.

'I don't want to lose my baby,' Emma burst out.

Matthew's eyes narrowed on her face.

'Of course not,' the nurse said soothingly, standing at the foot of the narrow bed.

But the nurse did not understand the situation, Emma thought. Nor did the doctor. How could they? The only person here who stood a chance of understanding how fraught she felt right now was Matthew. He ought to have been surprised by her abrupt change of heart. Perhaps even annoyed that she now wanted to keep the baby she had been fighting against for weeks. It was so contrary of her, so bloody-minded, she could not even understand it herself.

There was nothing in Matthew's face to show he was surprised though. Nothing but his usual, calm acceptance of her choice, whatever that choice might be.

Suddenly the sonic device pressed deeper, almost hurting her, and there was a strange kind of galloping sound. Like distant horses charging over a hill at speed.

The doctor smiled, her eyes brightening with obvious relief. 'There it is, Emma. Your baby's heartbeat. Strong and rhythmic too.' She listened to the galloping sound for another few seconds, then removed the Sonicaid. Her nod was one of complete satisfaction. 'That sounds perfectly healthy to me. Good news.'

'So that's what a baby's heartbeat sounds like,' Matthew

said. 'I'd always wondered.'

Emma could not find any words at first. She was reeling from having heard her baby's heartbeat at last. There had been a feeling of unreality about it since the first day she had missed her period. As though she might wake up at any minute and find the whole thing had been a dream. But that heartbeat was no dream. It was real. It was happening.

'I'm having a baby,' she told Matthew at last, and suddenly understood what that meant. The enormity of it all. 'Oh God.'

She was gripping his hand so hard that he winced.

'Sorry,' she whispered, and relaxed her grip.

'Don't worry about it.' Matthew smiled down at her, and she realised with a jolt that his eyes were misty. 'That was quite something, wasn't it? Another little heart, beating inside you.'

Penny waited while the nurse dried Emma's sticky tummy with some paper roll. 'I'll be in touch with the ultrasound department, to arrange for a full scan. Could you come back to the hospital this week? Say, tomorrow or the next day? I'm going to suggest they fit you in as soon as possible, so we can find out how far along you are.'

'I suppose that would be okay.' Emma frowned, a little worried now. Her heart was beating almost as fast as the baby's. 'But why the hurry? Is there a problem?'

'Not at all. But you do need some antenatal care.'

'So my funny turn today –'

'Won't have done the baby any harm at all. Though you need some blood tests to check your iron levels. You may be anaemic, which would explain the dizziness and reduced energy levels you've been experiencing.'

Emma nodded.

'Morning sickness may be taking its toll as well, especially if you've been skipping meals. You'll need to discuss proper nutrition with your primary care-giver at the antenatal clinic.' The doctor paused. 'Basically, it's important we perform a full scan. To assess how the baby is developing and work out your due date.'

'My due date,' Emma repeated slowly.

Matthew gave her a reassuring smile. 'Everything's going to be fine. I'll be there, you don't have to go through this alone.'

She looked back at him wonderingly. He had understood at once what she was thinking. That it was all happening too fast. That she had only really decided a few minutes ago to have this baby and raise it herself, and already the doctor was talking about scans and nutrition and due dates, which meant many months of pregnancy still ahead, and then the big moment itself, the actual day of giving birth.

And all that was so damn scary she could hardly think straight.

He searched her face. 'Unless you want to, of course. If I'm crowding you, just say the word and I'll go.'

She shook her head. 'No,' she whispered, and managed a tremulous smile. 'But only if you're sure.'

'Of course I'm sure.'

'But none of this is even ...' She glanced down at her tummy, relieved when the nurse began to pull her dress down and remove all the discreet paper coverings. She lowered her voice. 'Let's face it, it's not your fault I made such a mess of things and got myself pregnant.'

The nurse glanced at her, then at him, her face scrunched up in sudden disapproval. Like she was sucking a lemon.

It was obvious she thought Matthew was the father.

His eyes met hers with heavy irony. 'Shut up, okay? Not another word. I'm happy to be here with you. That's all that matters.'

Emma looked away from his too-observant gaze, suddenly a bit weepy. Pregnancy hormones again, she told herself and bit her lip to prevent the tears from coming.

But secretly she knew it wasn't only about hormones this time. Something else was happening inside her, in the region of her heart, not just her tummy.

She watched the doctor tapping away at the computer keyboard, trying to arrange a time for her scan. It was hard to stay calm with all these powerful new feelings coming at her – almost out of nowhere. She had been undecided when she got up this morning, unsure where her life was going. Now at least she knew what was going to happen in the immediate future, even if the details were still a little fuzzy.

'Thank you, Matthew.'

'For what?'

'For everything. For being …' Emma smiled, remembering the tiny galloping heartbeat they had both heard. 'Perfect.'

When Matthew did not respond, she glanced back at him. Instantly doubts assailed her. Had she said something wrong? He was still holding her hand, but his smile had vanished and he was looking troubled.

'Nobody's perfect,' he said.

CHAPTER FOURTEEN

'I don't need a wheelchair, honestly. I'm only trotting down to the little shop for a new colouring book.' Crystal touched her bare feet to the cool floor of the ward, and shivered despite the over-heated room. 'Five minutes, that's all.'

The nurse shook her head but did not argue. 'Slippers,' was all she said, and ducked to help Crystal slip them on. 'Now, take it easy. Or I'll be in trouble for letting you out of bed again. I don't want a repeat of last time.'

Last time, Crystal's brave but foolish attempt to reach the toilets without assistance had ended with her in a pathetic heap only a few feet from the ward door. After that incident, she had been threatened with a reintroduction of a catheter. Luckily, the very next morning her temperature had come right down, leaving her able to take solids again.

Not bad for someone who had almost died. According to the consultant who had seen her yesterday, at any rate.

'Yes, sister,' she said meekly, and saluted the nurse.

'You cheeky … Go on, get your colouring book then.' The nurse grinned. 'But I warn you, if you're not back within ten minutes, I'll send my minions in search of you.'

'You have minions?'

'And access to electric shock therapy.'

Crystal made a face. 'I'll be good, I promise.'

Freedom at last.

She shuffled carefully out of the ward and down the broad corridor, heading for the little shop. Soon she was regretting her decision. It had felt like an achievable mission while still lying on her back in bed, staring at the ceiling and bored to the point of oblivion. But now that she was on her feet, her body was whining to be back under the covers. Which was worrying, given the less than positive prognosis she had received during the past week in hospital.

She was not one hundred percent again yet, that was for sure. Not even fifty percent. Maybe not even thirty percent, if she was honest.

But surely she was not in serious danger of dying?

She was still off her food, though the doctors insisted she needed to eat more and build up her strength in anticipation of a transplant. She felt queasy despite a nearly empty stomach. And feverish without an actual fever.

'Your body's still recovering from the infection,' the consultant had decided with a brisk air, calling her occasional spasms of pain and shivering, 'after-shocks.' Like she was an earthquake zone. 'You need bed rest,' he had declared. 'Or you won't be fit for your transplant.'

Bed rest sounded great until you were actually undergoing it. Then it was the tedious activity – or rather, total absence of activity – in the universe. And Crystal hated being inactive, even for a few hours. Let alone long, lonely days on a hospital ward. Even the prospect of endless daytime television piped to a personal screen above her head had not made it more appealing.

She had asked the consultant, 'Can't I have bed rest at home?' but he had refused, ridiculously claiming she could have a relapse at any moment. 'We need you here where we can keep an eye on your vitals.'

My *vitals*, she thought ironically, supporting herself against the wall as she rested for a moment. They felt far from vital today. More like *inessentials*.

Her mum had visited every day, of course, bless her. And stayed by her bedside for several hours a day, despite having to leave the guesthouse unattended during that time. 'Oh, those surfers can take care of themselves,' she had said airily, dismissing Crystal's concerns. 'Shovel some eggs and bacon into them first thing, and they'll be fine on the beach all day. Their sheets and towels are all clean. They won't care if I'm there or not.'

But she had not seen Jack.

That worried Crystal far more than any number of sulky surfers ringing at the guesthouse reception and getting no response.

Emma had come in to see her that first day, and also a few days later, with Matthew in attendance both times, the pair of them looking radiant and troubled at the same time. So that relationship was definitely on. How serious it might be, she was unsure. There had been some talk of babies and scans, which had mostly gone over Crystal's head, though she had not missed Emma's air of consternation at the thought of giving birth. Everything was fine with the pregnancy, apparently, which the ultrasound technician had reckoned to be due in early February. She supposed the relationship must be complicated, what with Emma being pregnant, and Matthew liking her but perhaps not enough to contemplate raising another man's child as his own.

She had mentioned Jack.

Both Emma and Matthew had looked at her blankly. Jack had not been in touch, though apparently he had gone into the café and spoken to Boris on the day she had been taken ill.

So he knew she was in hospital.

'Oh goody,' Crystal had said. 'So now he must be absolutely sure he's been dating an invalid.'

Emma had opened her eyes wide at this admission. 'So you and Jack are *dating*, then? For definite?'

She had not known how to reply. In a way, her relationship with Jack was as on-and-off and tenuous as Emma's with Matthew. But maybe the fact that he had not visited her in hospital was a sign. A sign that her prospective boyfriend had finally seen sense and was not going to bother pursuing her any longer.

She tried to be happy about his absence. But she wasn't happy. She was bloody torn in two. Yes, she liked Jack. She was maybe even a bit in love with him, handsome and cheeky sod that he was. But she knew it was not fair to encourage him. Not when his last girlfriend had died just before the wedding, and she herself could keel over at any moment.

Reaching the little shop with her purse, she studied the colouring books on offer before selecting one that featured mountain views and cascading waterfalls, and promised the achievement of an almost Zen-like calm during the act of colouring.

She picked up a small pack of colouring pencils too, and carried both items to the till.

'I'll pay for those,' a voice said behind her. A deep, male voice. And wildly, tantalisingly familiar. 'And these chocolate bars, please.'

Crystal felt her heart thunder. Stay calm, she told herself. Don't look round at him.

The lady behind the counter rang up the sale, smiling at Jack with obvious admiration. Seriously, was there anyone who didn't think the man was good-looking?

'Hello, Jack.'

He smiled at Crystal, his dark eyes intent. 'Hello, Crystal.'

She ignored his offer and opened her purse, though her whole body was tingling with excitement that he had come to visit her at last. She could not let him see how she felt. It was too ridiculous, the idea of her starting any kind of relationship when she was so sick. She was actually in hospital, for goodness' sake. In her best striped pyjamas.

'It's good to see you. But I can't let you pay.'

'Nonsense, of course you can.' He was already calmly handing over his card. 'It's my pleasure. Anyway, I meant to buy you some new colouring books on the way here. But I was running a bit late, sorry.'

He punched his card number onto the keypad, then glanced sideways at her. There was something indefinable in that look.

'They're my colouring things,' she insisted. 'I should pay.'

'Don't be so bloody stubborn, woman.' He smiled at the sales assistant before helping Crystal out of the shop, his hand at her elbow. 'I should have known you wouldn't be looking after yourself, despite everything that's happened. I came looking for your ward, and instead find you stumbling about in your dressing gown and slippers like some old Dickensian character –'

'I beg your pardon?'

'I just couldn't believe my eyes when I recognised you. Who on earth let you out of bed?'

'Why shouldn't I be out of bed? Why does everyone keep trying to keep me in bed. There's nothing wrong with me.'

Jack caught her as she sagged suddenly, her traitorous legs giving way. 'Oh yes, I can see that. Which ward?'

Wordlessly, she pointed in the right direction.

Jack walked slowly alongside her, supporting her round the waist. She did not argue, enjoying the warmth of his arm, his hard hip banging against hers. She might be ill, but she was not dead yet.

The word 'yet' left her cold inside.

'Why did you come to see me?'

'I couldn't stay away.'

'Oh, really?' The pain in her heart momentarily got the better of her. 'If you couldn't stay away, then why haven't you come to see me before?'

'That's more complicated.'

'I can probably keep up if you use small words.'

'Your mum has been giving me daily reports on your progress,' he said hesitantly.

'That's not an answer.'

'I told you, it's complicated.'

'Oh, really? Actually, it sounds pretty simple to me.' Crystal tried hard but was unable to disguise the jealous pitch to her voice. 'What's her name?'

'You think I'm seeing someone else?'

'It makes sense.'

'The only thing that would make sense right now is if I were to bash you over the head with this bloody colouring book.'

'You're threatening me with violence?'

'I wanted to come, you little idiot. I was desperate to see you, to see with my own eyes that you were okay. As soon as I heard what had happened, I rang your mother to ask which ward you were in.' Jack's voice cracked with strain, and then abruptly deepened. 'She begged me not to visit you.'

'Oh, come on.'

He stopped walking, and she stopped too, staring up at him in disbelief. 'I'm sorry, but it's true. I tried to stay away, Crystal. Your mother said she didn't want you over-tired. That it would do more harm than good if you … If we saw each other before you were fully recovered and home again.'

'I'm going to strangle her,' Crystal said.

She took a few ill-advised steps forward, nearly colliding with a wall which she could have sworn had not been there a few seconds before.

'And she's probably right, judging by the bizarre way you're reacting.' Jack held her by both shoulders, looking down into her face. 'Just to be clear, I told myself to stay away from you until you were home again. And I meant to.

I don't want to be responsible for … for making this any worse than it already is.'

'So what changed your mind?'

'I couldn't stand it any longer. Not seeing you. Not being able to talk to you.' He paused, then swallowed hard. 'I'm in love with you, Crystal.'

She stared. 'Oh.'

'And I think you may be in love with me too.'

'Oh.'

Jack bent his head and kissed her.

The kiss took rather a long time, and after it was over, she rested her head on his shoulder with a contented smile.

'I'm serious,' he told her. 'I love you.'

'Oh,' she repeated, not terribly worried by the fact that her conversation had stopped making sense since he'd said he loved her.

He hugged her. 'Oh, indeed.'

'But what about my illness? The lupus?'

'What about it?'

'I could die.'

'So could I,' he pointed out coolly, 'if I forgot to look both ways crossing the road. Or for a hundred other reasons. Is that your only objection to me being in love with you? That you might die?'

'I suppose so.'

'Then it's not much of an objection, is it?'

She considered that, then gave a helpless shrug.

There was a kind of logic behind what he was saying. And while she could not entirely agree with his philosophy, she could not disagree with it either. And she certainly liked his thinking. No complaints there.

But she could tell from the question still lingering in his face that something other than dumb acquiescence was required.

'All right then, yes,' she said.

His eyes sought hers urgently. 'Yes … *what?*'

'Yes, I think I love you too.'

He smiled briefly, but there was a world of meaning in that smile. 'I'm glad to hear it. In that case, let's get you back to bed.'

Crystal pretended to be shocked. 'Jack, in a hospital?'

His eyes twinkled. But he ignored the bait.

'Come along, you saucy menace.' He slipped a supportive arm around her waist again. 'I'm not planning a seduction, as well you know. You need your rest, starting right now. No more trips to the shop, you hear me? No more wandering about the hospital in your slippers. Not until the doctor says it's safe.'

'I hate it when people fuss.'

'Then you're going to have to hate me for a little while,' he said firmly. His voice left her in no doubt about his feelings. 'No more arguments, Crystal. This is for your own good. Now I've got you, I don't intend to lose you.'

CHAPTER FIFTEEN

'Are you one hundred percent certain about this?' Emma asked Boris for about the third time as he placed the sign outside the café door.

'Of course I'm certain,' Boris repeated without any show of annoyance, his patience with damn-fool questions apparently inexhaustible. 'We're usually closed by six o'clock anyway. So I'm not losing business. The sign is just to stop nosy types knocking at the door.'

She looked dubiously at the sign, which read in large block capitals: SORRY, CAFÉ CLOSED: PRIVATE EVENT.

Boris ushered her back inside the café and locked the door behind them. It felt odd to be locked in, she thought, peering out at the people still wandering past. Like it was a top-secret political meeting. The Rebel Alliance, heavily armed with mandala designs and watercolour pencils. But she supposed being locked into the café for a meeting was better than being interrupted by evening surfers looking for pots of tea or ice creams.

Besides, everyone was there who had said they were turning up. And the café looked lovely, the white-washed space lit with spotlights and the soft orange rays of the evening sun striking through large west-facing windows. Beyond those windows she could see the white rollers of the Atlantic, majestic and rhythmic as they crashed onto the gritty sands of a North Cornwall bay. Above them stood rows of beach huts, each door a different colour, deepened by the glowing sun, and beyond that the cliffs, imposing and covered with rough grasses.

She could not think of a better place for the club to meet.

They had set several rectangular tables together in one corner, the same way the group had been arranged in the library, and the club members had drawn up chairs, making a cosy space for themselves. She had asked Harold to advertise the change of venue on the library noticeboard and, to her surprise, he had agreed.

A few members of the club had cried off, perhaps aware that she had been sacked and not entirely comfortable about it. She could not blame them. She would have been hesitant herself if she had not known the full story. And in fact, senior management had stepped in and offered to reinstate her, no doubt fearful of being sued for wrongful dismissal. But by then Emma had realised how much she hated having to work alongside people who had so little respect for her. So she had accepted six months' pay instead, and was 'considering her options' as she had told Harold.

But as she gazed around the room, she could see that the core of the colouring book club was there.

There was Jack, Fiona and Crystal – looking rather healthier now that she had been discharged from hospital – her own gorgeous Matthew and, of course, Boris himself, who had so kindly offered to host the club at his beach café until she found a more permanent home for it.

'Shall we make a start?' Emma asked happily.

The others looked at each other awkwardly. For a moment, nobody spoke. Then Fiona cleared her throat and stood up, holding something behind her back.

'First,' Fiona said, 'we have something to say to you, Emma.'

'*We?*'

'The members of the club.'

Emma felt worried, but tried not to show it. 'Go on.'

'Well,' Fiona began hesitantly, looking round at the others.

Then they all shouted 'Congratulations,' at the same time, and cheered loudly, making Emma jump.

'Congratulations on the baby,' Fiona finished, grinning at her surprise. She held out a brightly wrapped parcel. 'I hope you don't mind. I know you were keeping it quiet before. But since it's common knowledge now, we decided to club together to buy you a little something.'

'Oh goodness.'

'Go on, take it.'

Emma accepted the large parcel, gazing at her friends in astonishment. 'I don't know what to say. Except … thank you.'

Laughing at her expression, Matthew nodded to the gift. 'Go on, then. Open it.'

Still stunned by their thoughtfulness, she began to unwrap the parcel. The grinned as she realised what it was. A colouring book, and some very expensive-looking pencils. She turned them over. Swiss-made, professional quality, in a wide range of colours. Probably cost a fortune.

'These are lovely, thank you so much.' She turned to the colouring book itself, and gasped. 'Oh, this is perfect.'

It was a book of Cornish scenes, mostly beach and moorland, but with one beautiful picture of Truro Cathedral surrounded by narrow medieval lanes, all the pages intricately drawn and ready for colouring.

'Thank you,' she kept saying. 'What great friends you are.'

Boris drew out a chair for her to sit down. 'We thought about getting you baby clothes,' he admitted.

'Like a baby shower in the States,' Crystal added.

'But it's not easy to pick the right things for a new baby,' Boris continued, nodding. 'And since you've some time on your hands before the baby even arrives … and this is a colouring book club …'

'Honestly, I couldn't be happier. This is the best baby shower present I've ever had,' Emma told them.

'Not to mention being the only baby shower present you've ever had,' Matthew said drily.

'That too.' She laughed, and sat down at last, gesturing Fiona to do the same. She could feel heat in her cheeks, and not just because of the way Matthew was looking at her. Though the warmth in his eyes was not helping. 'Well, having thoroughly embarrassed me, I think the least you can all do is start colouring.'

'Not much fun, is it?' Crystal winked at her across the table. 'Being the centre of attention.'

Emma smiled ruefully at her friend. 'Not much. Though when it brings me presents as fabulous as these, I'm not about to complain.'

She was glad to see Crystal looking so well, even though she had only been out of hospital for a week now. They were sharing Crystal's bedroom at the guesthouse, but Fiona had promised that, as soon as the summer season was over, Emma could move into one of the larger second floor rooms – and stay there as long as she wanted. There would be rent to pay, of course, once she was no longer sharing with Crystal. Emma had insisted on that, despite Fiona's generosity. But she was getting on top of her financial situation, especially now she'd received a severance payment from the library.

Matthew had offered to help out too, the darling man. But while that was lovely of him, and much appreciated, she wanted to stand on her own two feet if she could. As soon as the baby was old enough for nursery, she intended to go back to work. Until then, she would find a way to manage somehow.

With the help of her friends.

Boris played some music on the café sound system. Soft mood music that was not too distracting for the colourers, but made a pleasant background while they worked.

Fiona looked up at him, pleased. 'Oh, I like this song.'

'I know,' Boris said.

Fiona smiled, and looked away. But Emma noticed that Crystal's mum seemed a bit pink-cheeked. And not from too much sun. Was there a romance going on under their noses between Boris and Fiona?

Everyone chose a book and a picture that suited their mood. Then the club fell to colouring in a companionable silence, occasionally discussing the weather or the local news.

Emma tried hard to concentrate on her lake full of swans, but she kept looking across the table at Matthew.

Sometimes he too glanced up from his science fantasy colouring book – he'd chosen a gorgeous spread of dragons in flight for that week's project – and caught her eye. Then her heart beat hard and she had to look away, as Fiona had done with his dad. Meeting his gaze so directly felt like too intimate an act in public.

Could this thing really work out between them?

Matthew believed so, despite the fact that she was carrying another man's child. Perhaps she ought to have a little more faith too.

Boldly, next time their eyes met, Emma smiled at him, and he smiled back. A flicker of flame leapt between them.

Oh goodness.

It was so tempting to think ahead to after the club meeting, when Matthew had promised to take her out for a walk along the headland. She felt sure there would be kissing. Which was probably not the most calming thought to have while colouring in a lake, she thought with a sigh, glancing down at one of her swimming swans, now marred by an ugly blue streak on its otherwise immaculate wing.

'Oops,' she said.

Matthew frowned, looking to see what she had done. Then gave her a knowing smile. 'Not got your mind on your work tonight?'

'Shut up.'

But she was grinning too.

Halfway through the meeting, someone rattled the café door. Then knocked on the glass.

Emma glanced round at the door. There was a woman outside the café. Tall, well-built, bleach-blonde hair down her back, with a small child squirming in her arms. A fair-haired toddler, by the look of it. Emma had the feeling she'd seen the woman before at the library story-telling sessions for under-fives. One of Carmen's friends.

'Boris,' she said softly.

His shaven head was gleaming under the café spotlights, bent over his colouring book. He was colouring in the picture of a rusting old hulk in a harbour of rusting old hulks, with apparent absorption.

'Boris,' she repeated, more loudly.

Boris jerked, then looked up. 'Sorry, what?'

'There's someone at the door.'

Matthew was reaching under the table for a lost pen. 'Don't worry, Dad, I'll get it,' he said, his voice muffled.

Boris was annoyed. 'Tell them it's a private event. I put a sign out there, for God's sake.'

Fiona craned her neck to see the woman at the door. 'She's got a kiddy with her. He probably needs the loo.'

'There are public toilets only a few hundred metres down the road,' Boris pointed out, then shrugged when Fiona pursed her lips in disapproval. 'Look, people are always asking for the loo here. Drives me crazy. They don't even buy anything, just come in to use the facilities.'

'It's okay, Dad, I'll show her where the other toilets are. They really aren't far.' Matthew was already heading across to the door with long, easy strides. Then he faltered.

Emma looked round in surprise, watching him. What was wrong?

'Oh bloody hell.' Boris had got to his feet, staring.

After a brief hesitation, Matthew unlocked the door and went outside. She heard him speaking to the woman in quiet, even tones. But the woman replied in a raised voice, oddly shrill and growing shriller by the moment. Was she going to demand entrance to the café? Barge in here, perhaps?

Emma was cross at first, but then remembered her own condition. Soon she would be the mother of a small child herself. And it must be awful to be stuck in the middle of nowhere with a toddler demanding the toilet urgently.

Still, that was no excuse for the rude woman to yell at Matthew like that.

The woman put down the toddler, who said something loudly and tugged on Matthew's jeans.

Then the woman turned and stalked away, leaving her child behind.

'Goodness me,' Fiona said, tutting. 'She's surely not going to leave her child behind. Well, what a bad mother.'

Boris said nothing. But he looked unhappy.

To her astonishment, Matthew did not come back inside though. On the contrary, he took the small child's hand and followed the woman down the road a little way.

'Chelsea,' he called her after her as he passed one of the open café windows. 'Chelsea, you can't do this. Come back.'

Emma caught her breath in sudden, terrible comprehension.

Chelsea.

That was the name of Matthew's wife. Or rather, his would-be ex. The one he was suing for divorce.

But if the blonde was Chelsea, *then whose child was that?*

Boris followed his son outside.

Speechless, Emma watched the two men talking urgently over the head of the fair-haired toddler, a small boy in blue shorts and a white T-shirt. The boy was crying now, a dismal wail that struck at Emma's heart and made her want to weep herself.

Could that toddler be Matthew's son?

Why had he never mentioned that he had a child with Chelsea? He must have known it would have made a difference to her. If she had known about the boy, she would never have considered Matthew to be free to have a relationship with her, given that she too was pregnant. Once a child was involved, things became too horribly complicated to contemplate. He must know that, as a parent himself.

He had abandoned one marriage and child, and was now planning to hook up with another pregnant woman, even though the child wasn't his. Perhaps he was one of these serial father-figures her mum used to complain about when reading aloud from the newspapers, men who deliberately 'collected' children so they could reap a crop of child benefit payments and never have to work themselves.

Matthew did not seem that kind of person though. He was not like that, she told herself, not in any way calculating.

Yet he had not mentioned that little boy.

Fiona and Crystal were looking at her with pity in their eyes. Maybe they too had guessed what was going on.

Oh God.

Emma bent her head and tried to colour in the bulrushes beside the lake, choosing a vivid dark green pencil from the packet of Swiss pencils. It was a lovely shade, perfect for the picture. But her hand was trembling too much and she could not stay within the lines.

With a quiet sob, more like a hiccup really, she gave up and stuffed the expensive new pencil back in the packet.

What a bloody mess this was.

She felt like dying.

Matthew had returned the child to its mother now, and was coming back into the café with Boris, his normally cheerful face strained and pale.

'Sorry about that,' he said, coming back to the colouring table, but did not meet Emma's eyes.

'Everything okay, Matthew?' Fiona asked him, not bothering to disguise her curiosity.

'Mum, hush,' Crystal hissed.

'Fine,' Matthew said, with a quick, harassed smile in her direction. But although Fiona smiled back, it was clear nobody believed him. 'Absolutely fine.'

Boris put a hand on his son's shoulder. Matthew ducked his head, and Boris removed the hand slowly.

Emma winced at the jagged shard of glass pressing into her heart. Or at least that's how it felt to her. She held back tears with difficulty.

'Here,' Boris said gruffly, pushing the plate of biscuits towards him. 'Have a biscuit, son.'

Matthew took a jammy dodger. But he did not eat it. Instead, he put it down next to his picture of dragons, and made a show of selecting the right pencil to continue colouring.

There was an awkward silence.

Emma sat there for a long while, not colouring anymore, just staring at her swans. She felt humiliated and more hurt than she had ever been before. Even her parents' desertion over the pregnancy had not wounded her like this terrible lie Matthew had told by omission.

She wanted to walk out the door.

Yet how could she?

This was her club. *The Colouring Book Club*. She was the founder member. She could not walk out. And it would be intolerably rude too, after everything Boris had done to ensure its survival as a club.

She could not let his lie go unchallenged though. That would make her the worst kind of coward, somehow who sees perfectly well what's going on, yet says and does nothing.

She struggled to find her voice. It was important to

appear only casually interested, she told herself. Inside she knew she would fail miserably though. This meant everything to her. *The truth* meant everything.

'Matthew?'

He did not look up from his colouring. 'Yes?'

'Was that blonde woman your ex?'

'Yes.'

'Chelsea?'

'Yes.'

Now she really wanted to cry. Her voice was a dry rasp in her throat. 'And the little boy?'

'That was Tyler.' His head was still bent over his pencils. 'Her son.'

She shot him a furious look, her eyes flashing with unshed tears. 'Yet you sent them away.' Her temper was about to crack, so she kept her voice low. She was very aware of the others listening as they coloured, but could not help herself from adding, 'You didn't need to do that. Not on my account.'

He looked up at her, surprise in his eyes. 'It wasn't on your account. Though it's true to say that things with Chelsea are … complicated.'

'I bet.'

His surprise deepened. 'Emma …'

'Forget it,' she said sharply, and closed her colouring book. 'I'm sorry, I'm not feeling too great.' She looked at Crystal's mum. 'Fiona, do you mind if I walk back alone to the guesthouse?'

'Do what you like, love.' Fiona's eyes widened. 'You've got your key, haven't you?'

Emma nodded, and got up, gathering her things.

After a moment's silence, Matthew too stood up. His face was like stone. 'I'll walk with you.'

'No,' she told him, her voice harsh with unshed tears. Everyone looked at her, and she forced herself to sound saner, more reasonable. 'That is, thank you but I'd rather be alone. I'm fine, I'm just not in the mood for …'

She could not finish.

Boris went to unlock the door for her.

'Thanks,' she told him a little unevenly, and slipped out into the warm and golden evening sunshine, her colouring presents tucked under her arm. It was still so bright by the sea that her eyes started to water; she wiped at her cheeks ineffectually, her head bent. 'I'm sorry for causing you any trouble.'

'No trouble,' Boris told her, but she could see the heavy frown in his eyes and knew that he was still unhappy. 'And no need to apologise, Emma. You take care of yourself, you hear me?'

'Of course,' she said, then added in a stilted voice, 'Take care of yourself and Matthew, would you?'

Without waiting to hear his reply, Emma turned her face away from the glory of the setting sun and started to walk.

CHAPTER SIXTEEN

'So what do you think?' Jack asked in a whisper, lying on his back next to her. He sounded confident, cocky even. But Crystal knew deep down how fragile that confidence could be. 'Be honest with me, okay?'

'It's too big.'

'What?'

'It'll never fit.'

'Now you're being ridiculous,' he told her, but she knew he was worried she might be right. 'Look at it. It's the perfect size.'

'No,' Crystal insisted, her tone emphatic, and shook her head. 'It's far too big and far too shiny.'

'Shiny?' Jack sounded stunned now.

'I'm sorry. I'm an honest person. I can only tell you the truth.' She threw her arms wide in a gesture of defeat. 'I can't go round *dazzling* people all day. Which, let's face it, I could hardly avoid with a honking great thing like that on my finger.'

There was a long pause while Jack absorbed that information. Then he sat up on the grass and looked at her searchingly.

Below them, the Atlantic rose and fell in its age-old dance in and out of the ancient harbour at Boscastle. It was a beautiful sunny day and Jack had borrowed a friend's car, as he did not own one himself, and driven them down the coast of North Cornwall for a day out.

A very *special* day out, she realised now.

'This is a joke, right?' he asked in severe tones. 'You're not being serious. You *can't* be serious. You're pulling my leg.'

Crystal was only able to hold her blank expression for another ten seconds. Then she collapsed, laughing.

She held out the ring box he had offered her as they lay there on the grassy slopes together. 'Of course I'm joking,' she managed to gasp. 'This ring is utterly, unspeakably … *impossibly* perfect for me. In fact, it's the most perfect engagement ring I've ever seen in my life.'

His eyes narrowed. 'Hold on a minute,' he said suspiciously, 'is this the *only* engagement ring you've ever seen in your life?'

Crystal bit her lip. 'Busted.'

'You …'

'Hey,' she said, and beat off his sudden attack.

His warm arms came around her, his face very close to hers, blocking out that idyllic view of the ocean and the ancient, algae-green walls of Boscastle harbour.

'But you genuinely like it? And it's *not* too big?'

'You're the one who must be joking now. I love it to bits, Jack. How could you think I wouldn't like something that stunning?'

Carefully, she put down the ring box, since he was unwilling to take it back, and took his face in both hands instead. Then she leant forward and kissed him on the lips. Even though they were in full view of ramblers straggling down the nearby cliff path into the harbour, Jack did not resist. Quite the opposite, in fact. All the same, it took a little while before she was completely satisfied with their kiss, which left her very warm and flushed, and him a little dazed-looking, despite the cool breezes sweeping in off the Atlantic Ocean.

'That's how much I like it,' she told him deeply. 'In fact, I like it a lot more than that. But the doctor said I had to avoid getting too excited, so I can only show you a tenth of what I'm feeling. That good enough for you?'

'It's a start.'

She shook her head. 'Oh Jack.'

'Don't blame me if I fall for your stunts. You're too convincing. Besides,' Jack added, 'how can I be sure you're not right about the ring not fitting? It looked about the right size in the shop. But you haven't tried it on yet.'

Crystal met his gaze, and could not help smiling. Just looking at Jack made her smile. She eased the gorgeous engagement ring out of its velvet-lined case and slipped it onto her finger. Exactly as she had anticipated, and Jack had cleverly guessed, it fitted. It was maybe a tiny bit loose, given how much weight she had lost in recent months. But as soon as she was well enough to eat properly again, she intended to make up for that.

Five lush emeralds winked up at her as she turned her finger this way and that, admiring how beautiful the ring looked.

'Perfect,' she said softly.

She looked down at the view of the sea rolling through the dog-leg entrance to Boscastle Harbour, its huge heavy turquoise swell crowding into that narrow space. How many thousands of lovers had climbed the cliff path to admire this view together, she wondered? It was certainly a perfect spot for being given a perfect engagement ring.

Sighing with happiness, she lay back on the grass, enjoying the warmth of sunshine on her face. She had become a little weary on the long walk from the car park, it was true. But with Jack supporting her every step of the way, she had not felt that tired at all. Not the way she used to feel tired before she met him and joined the colouring book club. That hopeless fatigue that was so impossible to shake off, where everything felt like an effort and the sky always looked grey.

And there had been so much to see in Boscastle itself, this old-fashioned little village one of her favourite places on the north coast of Cornwall. The shops and cafés were all open for the season, and there were smiling walkers everywhere, with sticks and rucksacks, and children playing noisily in the harbour shallows near the old fish houses. Fishing nets and lobster pots had been stored for mending along the approach track, and there were a few small boats bobbing gently in the inner harbour.

The little fishing village felt alive.

She felt alive.

'So?' Jack asked, the words breaking into her thoughts.

'So what?'

'Don't tease.'

Crystal wrinkled her nose, then looked at him. 'Erm, what was the question again?'

His eyes flashed with sudden laughter. 'You ...'

'Honestly, I've forgotten.' She tapped her forehead, frowning in a sad, perplexed manner. 'It's my condition. It affects my brain. Who are you?'

Jack bit his lip. His face became more sober. 'The question was, will you marry me, you annoying scamp?'

'Oh, that.'

'Yes, that.' He was looking at her intently now. 'So?'

It was time to put him out of his misery. And let her into this magical golden spell of happiness.

'So the answer is yes. You know it is.'

Jack gave a strangled whoop, then punched the air.

She pretended to be concerned, staring at him. 'Are you okay? Should I call an ambulance? I know a really good consultant ...'

'Shut up.'

They kissed again, this time for very much longer.

When Crystal sat up a while later, gently breaking free of Jack's warm, enclosing arms, there was grass in her hair and she felt all muzzy. Like she'd been asleep. But of course she had been very much awake. And having the most delicious time.

'Oh Jack,' she said again, happily.

The Atlantic Ocean made an odd buzzing noise.

She frowned.

Jack, who had been picking grass out of her hair, frowned too. 'What's that?'

She listened, head on one side, thoroughly confused. The buzzing noise continued. Suddenly she realised it was coming from beneath them, not from the ocean. From under the picnic mat, in fact.

'My phone,' she said abruptly.

She unearthed the mobile. It was her mother.

There were several text messages waiting to be read, and three missed calls that must have come in unnoticed while they were picnicking.

Crystal answered it, frowning. 'Mum?'

'Crystal, thank God. Where on earth are you?' She sounded panicked. 'I've been trying to reach you for the past twenty minutes. You've got to come home straight away.'

'Slow down, Mum. I'm in Boscastle with Jack. Why do I need to come home? What's happened?'

'The hospital called, love. Half an hour ago now. That's why I've been trying to get hold of you.'

Crystal turned to stare at Jack. Her breath had suddenly caught in her throat.

He saw her expression and his brows twitched together. 'What's wrong?' he mouthed, staring back at her.

But she could not answer him. Not yet. Instead she reached out and grabbed his hand, squeezing it without explanation.

Her heart began to beat faster. *Oh God, was this it?*

'The hospital?' she repeated blankly.

'The transplant team. They want to know where you are.' Her mum was breathless. 'They're sending a helicopter.'

'A helicopter?'

'They've found a donor. A good match.' Fiona gulped. 'Darling, there's not much time. The team's being called in right now. They want you at the hospital and prepped for surgery within the next couple of hours, or the whole thing's off.'

Crystal stumbled to her feet, sick with apprehension. She stared out over the ocean. Suddenly the sea, so beautiful before, looked bleak and hostile.

'Tell me what I need to do.'

She wasn't sure how she got through the next few minutes of the conversation, her heart was hammering so hard. Yet somehow she managed to end the call without giving away her anxiety and making her mum feel a thousand times worse.

The mobile phone clenched in her hand, she turned to Jack. From the look on his face, it was clear he had a fair idea idea what was happening.

'They've located a liver for you,' he said, nodding.

'Yes.'

'But that's fantastic news. What's wrong?'

Crystal said nothing.

'You're going to get your transplant.' Jack took her in his arms. His voice in her ear should have been reassuring. 'This means you get another shot at life, a second chance you absolutely deserve. I couldn't be happier for you.'

Her mind was racing. 'There's a helicopter on its way. It has to happen now.'

'You're scared.'

Again, she said nothing.

'Hey, look at me.' When she turned her face towards him, Jack kissed her on the lips. 'I can be there with you the whole time, if you like. When you go to sleep, and when you wake up.'

'If I wake up.'

His eyes registered fear for a second. The same fear she was experiencing at the thought of undergoing such complicated surgery. Then he shook his head.

'You'll wake up,' he told her firmly. 'Even if I have to give you the kiss of life.'

She smiled, her responses on automatic. But it was becoming harder to focus on anything but what she had to do next. And shock had started to set in. Her legs were trembling. She felt cold and dizzy, despite the sunshine. The doctors had warned her this might happen. She was scared, Jack was right. But there was guilt churning inside her too. Awful, gut-wrenching guilt.

'Hey,' he said softly, 'I told you, don't worry. I'll be there for you. And so will your mum, I'm sure.'

He lifted her hand and kissed it lingeringly, the old-fashioned gesture reminding her what was on her finger. The beautiful emerald ring he had bought her. They were engaged now. It should have been the happiest day of her life. Instead, she felt like everything was about to end.

'What is it?' he asked.

'It's all happening too fast.' She blinked, not able to meet his gaze. 'I can't ... can't keep up.'

'That's not what's bothering you.'

He was so astute, it was as though he could read her mood, if not her actual mind.

'No, it's not,' she admitted.

He stroked the hair back from her forehead. 'What, then?'

'We don't have time. The helicopter –'

'Crystal, please tell me the truth. This isn't you worrying about not waking up, is it?'

'I am scared about the operation, yes.' She closed her eyes briefly, then admitted, 'But the worst thing is, someone out there has just died, and I'm supposed to be happy about it. Because their death could mean ...'

'Your life.'

She nodded, looking at him. 'It's so selfish. Somewhere out there, somebody has just heard their loved one has died. That they've lost their child, or wife, or parent. And I … I'm going to benefit from that loss. Tell me, how can I be happy about something that awful?'

'You can't be,' he agreed, his expression sober for once. 'You're right, Crystal. Somebody has died, and that's a tragedy. After Beverley died, I … I thought I'd never smile again. It was like losing the best part of myself. But at least this way their death gets to mean something. To have some kind of purpose. I didn't get to feel that way about Beverley. She wasn't an organ donor. But this person was, and that means part of them will live on in you.'

She stared at him. She had never thought of it like that before.

Jack kissed her again, then gave her a hug so tight it nearly drove the breath from her body.

'Now come on, let's get you to that helicopter before you run out of time.'

Emma reached the door by the third ring of the doorbell.

She was a little out of breath after having hurried all the way down from the top floor room where she had been vacuuming the carpets.

Nonetheless, she dragged off her work pinny, tidied her hair in the hall mirror, and tried to look professional and welcoming. She had been left in charge of the guesthouse during Crystal and Fiona's absence at the hospital. The least she could do for her friends at such a worrying time was to keep their business ticking over without any major incidents.

There was a ready smile on her face as she threw open the door.

All she could see was an absolutely vast bunch of flowers, so large it almost filled the doorway. The bunch contained romantic red roses in full bloom, white-throated lilies, lady's mantle, pretty carnations, a few green handfuls of fern.

The flowers looked and smelt gorgeous. Her smile faded somewhat. She had expected to find a would-be guest on the step, not half a florists' shop, lovely though that was.

She stared, mystified. 'Hello?'

The huge bunch of flowers was lowered to reveal Matthew. There was a smile on his face too, but she could tell he was far from cheerful. 'Hello.'

'You.'

'Can I come in?'

Matthew.

Her heart was thudding now. She could hardly take her eyes off him, he was such a welcome sight. But equally she could not forget Chelsea, his ex, and that cute little boy. They deserved better than the way he was treating them.

'I'm sorry, no.'

He put out a hand, stopping her from closing the door. 'At least listen to what I have to say before you kick me out.'

'You're not in,' she pointed out.

'Well, kick me off the premises then.' He glanced past her. 'No Fiona? I expected her to be the one to shoo me off the step.'

She took a deep breath, then realised she was being ridiculous. He was no danger to her. And this was hardly a conversation she wanted to have on the doorstep. Especially when a real guest might turn up at any minute.

'Okay, you'd better come in,' she said, not bothering to disguise her reluctance, and opened the door wider. 'But only for a few minutes.'

'Of course.'

'Five minutes, to be precise,' she told him sternly.

'Whatever you say.'

At least he was not arguing with her, she thought, and inexplicably felt a little disappointed by that. As though she would rather have had a humdinger of a fight with him.

Which was absolutely not the case.

Matthew followed her into Fiona's gleaming kitchen, and stood looking about blankly at the clean surfaces. Everything had been cleared away since breakfast, probably in the wrong places, given that it was Emma who had done all the cooking and the loading of the dishwasher and the clearing away in her friends' absence.

But at least the hard work was keeping her busy. Too busy to sit down and cry about the appalling mess she had made of her life.

'Have you got a vase?'

'I don't know, it's not my kitchen. I don't know my way round it yet.'

'They need to be put in water.' He studied the vast bouquet dubiously. 'Perhaps we could stand them in the sink in some water.'

She followed him to the sink.

Their eyes met.

It was hard to stand so close to him, to breathe in his warm scent, and not remember …

'I'm not sure Fiona would like that. It doesn't sound very hygienic.' But she did not have the first clue where to look for a vase, turning slowly on her heel as she surveyed the kitchen. 'Erm, maybe there's a vase in one of the lower cupboards? How about this one, under the sink?'

They both bent to the cupboard together, and cracked foreheads.

'Bloody hell.' She reeled back, her vision blurred.

Matthew swore rather more obscenely, clutching his temples as though in acute pain. Then grimaced. 'Sorry, that just slipped out.'

She seized the bouquet and thrust it into the sink. The overwhelming scent of lilies assailed her, redolent of grief and love and loss, and she could have wept.

'Are these for Crystal?' she asked.

He frowned. 'For Crystal? No, why on earth … ?'

'You haven't heard, then?'

'Tell me.'

So Emma told him about the liver donor that had been found for Crystal, and how a helicopter had come to whisk her and Fiona and Jack away to a hospital in the Midlands where the transplant team was waiting.

And that she had heard nothing from any of them since yesterday evening, when Crystal had gone into surgery.

By the time Emma finished her story, she was in floods of tears, her head bent, quite unable to make good sense anymore. And Matthew was standing a good deal closer than he had been at the start.

'Haven't heard a solitary thing … Crystal could have … Pegged out … And I don't know what to … No vases.'

Matthew made an abrupt noise under his breath. He pressed a clean tissue into her hand, and then dragged her into his arms.

'Come here.'

'No, I can't. You and Chelsea …'

'Forget that.'

'How can I forget it? You two have got a child together. A gorgeous little boy.' She cried out in pain at the memory of what she had seen at the café, her face buried against his chest. 'Oh, why didn't you tell me about him, Matthew? It's as though having a child doesn't matter to you at all. Like he means nothing. Poor little thing.'

Matthew stood immobile for a moment. Then he said slowly, 'I didn't tell you about Tyler because I was ashamed.'

'Ashamed of your son? Oh my God, you monster.'

'No, not ashamed of Tyler. I would never be ashamed of Tyler, never say or think such a thing. How the hell can you accuse me of …?' His chest heaved against her, and she looked up, staring in astonishment. Because Matthew was crying too. Crying openly, tears running down his cheeks. 'I'm ashamed of myself, for God's sake.'

'For leaving Chelsea with a baby?'

'No, no.' He tore her damp tissue in half, and dabbed at his face with his half. Not very successfully. 'For making such a fool of myself over her. For not believing what everyone was telling me.'

'I don't understand.'

'Chelsea was my wife. I had to stand by her, regardless, and to punch out any of my mates who dared say anything against her. That's what my dad taught me, that's what he said a married man should do. Complete loyalty is what a marriage is all about.' He swallowed hard. 'And that's exactly what Chelsea was relying on.'

She frowned, then stood back. 'Let me go.'

'Please …'

'Let me go, Matthew.'

His arms fell away, releasing her. 'I'm sorry,' he said.

'Tell me,' she said.

He shook his head, though from the tormented look in his eyes she was sure he was dying to spill everything.

'Emma, I can't. And it wouldn't do either of us any good to hear it. It's ancient history now.' He ran a hand across his face, apparently embarrassed by his unexpected show of emotion. He was getting himself back in control, shutting away those long-buried feelings. 'Besides, what happens between a man and wife should be private.'

Oh no, she was not going to accept that kind of reasoning. Not when their own happiness was at stake. Not to mention the happiness of her own unborn child.

'Tell me what happened between you and Chelsea, or you and I are finished forever.' She pulled out a kitchen chair and sat down on it, staring at him. 'And don't dare leave anything out.'

Matthew looked at her, then slowly nodded. He sat down opposite her and took her hand, staring down at it. Then he began to tell her, carefully and probably with many omissions, the story of his marriage to Chelsea.

'We were deeply in love,' he said, and even smiled, but the smile was short-lived. 'Chelsea is a free spirit though, and love wasn't enough to hold her. I should have seen that from the start, not tried to pin her down with marriage. In the end, she wanted more than I could offer her.' He frowned. 'More than love and adoration.'

Shortly after they were married, Chelsea had started going out pubbing and clubbing in the evenings with her friends. He had gone with her too at first, but he had been working long hours and eventually let her go out without him. Then she started to stay out all night, claiming that she was with a girlfriend. Still he had suspected nothing.

Then she had told him she was pregnant, even though they had decided to wait for a family. He had been using protection, so he was quite shocked. But pleased too. 'I thought it was mine, you see,' he said dully. 'My child. A miracle, the baby who wanted to be born.'

Emma looked at him with pity, already guessing the truth. 'It wasn't yours though.'

'It was one of our neighbours on the estate where we'd been living. I'd met him a few times at the pub. He and Chelsea …' Matthew shook his head, unable to continue with that thought. He sat up straighter, changed the subject. 'She didn't tell me until she was nearly due. We'd had a row, and I guess she wanted to hit out at me. Hurt me any way she could.'

'Oh God.'

'It worked too. I was in pieces.' He drew a long breath. 'But afterwards, when I'd calmed down, I told her it didn't matter so long as she still loved me. I wanted to hold our marriage together.'

'But she wasn't interested?'

'She left me a few days later. The guy was married but left his wife to be with Chelsea. A few weeks ago, he changed his mind though. Went back to his wife, said he didn't want anything to do with Chelsea or the kid. Oh, he's going to pay child maintenance, don't worry. He can't get away without doing that. But Chelsea's on her own again now.'

Emma held her breath. 'I see.'

'She says she wants us to try living together again. That Tyler needs a proper daddy, not a paper daddy, even if that man's not his actual biological father. Someone who'll play with him, look after him, take him out to the park, you know. Not a dad who pays child support but never bothers to see him.'

'You, in other words.'

He nodded. 'That's what you witnessed at the beach café. What you misunderstood, though I can see why you did. It must have looked bad. Chelsea was trying to leave Tyler with me, to make me guilty enough to ask her back to live with me again.' He looked sick. 'Poor bloody kid.'

'That's appalling.'

'It's par for the course with Chelsea. She hates to be pinned down, like I said. By a child or a lover. So she's looking for someone who'll take the responsibility off her shoulders. She never intended to be a single parent, and she hates it.'

Emma looked away, feeling guilt twist inside her. Soon she would be a single parent too. She only hoped she was ready for that responsibility.

'And now?'

'I can't go back to our marriage, even for Tyler's sake. He's a great kid and I wish him well. But I told her, it's too late for us to go back. The divorce papers are almost through. And besides, I'm …'

He looked at her intently.

'You're?'

'I'm in love with someone else.'

Her gaze locked with his. It was as though he could see right inside her, to the deep-buried need burning a hole in her heart. She did not know what to say. But she knew what she needed. For him to hold her and never let her go.

'Wh … who?'

'Emma, you know it's you.'

His eyes were still fixed on hers, she could not look

away. 'Even after the way I turned my back on you?'

'I don't blame you for that. You saw what Chelsea wanted you to see. Besides, it was my fault that happened. I was a fool. When she first got in touch to say she wanted to give our marriage another chance, I made a terrible mistake. I couldn't make her see that it was impossible, so I told her about us.' His voice deepened. 'About you.'

'Oh my God.'

'I didn't tell her your name. Or anything about the baby. I just said you were a member of the colouring book club.' He shrugged. 'Once Chelsea realised why I wasn't interested anymore, she got angry. Really angry. I'm fairly certain that's why she came to the café that evening. To force the issue … and maybe also trick you into thinking we'd had a kid together.'

'Impressive trick. It nearly worked.'

'It did work, didn't it?'

She felt awful. But she could not lie to him. 'Yes.'

'You never wanted to see me again, did you?'

'No.'

'So now you know the truth.'

She stood up clumsily, half-laughing at the irony of it all. 'The truth.' She shook her head when he stood up too and held out his hands to her. 'No, wait. I know the truth about Chelsea and Tyler. But you don't know the truth about this baby inside me. Because I don't know either. And we'll never know unless I find out who the father is.'

'I don't care about that. As far as I'm concerned, that baby is a part of you, and I love you. So I love that baby. No questions asked.'

'And can you be sure you'll always feel that way? Even if …' She could hardly get the words out. 'Even if we do find him one day? Because I'm going to keep on trying, I hope you realise that. I owe it to my child to keep trying. One day he or she might need to know who their biological father is.'

'There are no guarantees in life,' he said simply. 'My

first marriage taught me that. But I'm in love with you, Emma, and I'm more than willing to give this a go if you are.'

She was willing, and her eyes admitted that. This time Emma did not resist when Matthew came towards her, but turned up her face for his kiss.

He touched her shoulders lightly, as though afraid to break her, and said, 'I love you.'

'I love you too,' she told him.

Their lips met and she closed her eyes, happier than she had been for a very long time. His muscular arms felt like bulkheads around her, enclosing and protecting her for as long as she needed them.

Once she might have found that idea alarming.

But Emma knew she only had to say the word and Matthew would let go, freely give her whatever space she needed. Because she did need space. Space to be herself and never to forget who she was inside.

She needed love too though. As much as he could give her.

And the baby.

A really long while later, though they had no idea how much time had passed since they started kissing, the phone rang, startling them both out of their reverie.

Emma gazed around the kitchen for the telephone. The handset was lying on the side near the sink where she had left it earlier. She knew that she ought to answer it before the answerphone cut in. It could be an important call, maybe a reservation by a potential guest.

But she felt lost and dazed from his kisses, like she was in a dream, and her stupid feet refused to move.

She looked mutely at Matthew for help, who understood at once and answered the phone for her.

He spoke for a few minutes in a low voice, his back turned away. Then he said, 'Yes, of course,' and held out the phone to Emma. 'She wants to talk to you. Says it's urgent.'

'Who is it?'

'Fiona.'

'Oh.' Reality rushed back in like a cold tide and Emma straightened, holding the phone to her ear. 'Hello? Fiona?'

'I'm so sorry I didn't call before now. But it's been crazy here, Emma. We've barely slept since we arrived.' Fiona sounded exhausted. 'I'm here with Jack now. He says hi.'

'Say hi back to him for me.' Emma gripped the phone tightly, suddenly nervous for her friend. 'But, Fiona, how's everything going? What's … what's happened?'

'It's the best news possible.' She could hear the smile in Fiona's voice. 'The transplant operation is over, and Crystal's awake.'

EPILOGUE

The registrar herself came out to wave them goodbye from the doorway of the Victorian red brick building where they had finally been married.

'Good luck,' she called after them. 'Erm, not too much confetti, please.' Someone scattered confetti over her head, and she smiled wanly. 'Oh … well. Enjoy yourselves.'

The congregation crowded out onto the pavement too. It was a gorgeous spring day in Cornwall, and several people were already throwing handfuls of white confetti that looked exactly like cherry blossom over the happy couple. Small children ran shrieking and laughing between the emerging people, tripping up more than one person.

A driver in a passing car beeped her horn and waved frantically. The bride waved back, giggling.

The photographer tried in vain to corral the wedding party together for a few photographs. 'Over here in the garden, please,' he was calling above the noise. 'Family photographs first.'

And the warm May sun shone benignly on all their heads as it had been shining the whole week.

'I can't believe they beat us to it,' Crystal said, watching this circus with a happy smile on her face.

Jack grinned, and wrapped his arm tight about her waist. 'Hey, not long to wait though. What is it, five weeks?'

'Almost to the day. Do you regret waiting?'

'I don't regret anything.'

'I wanted a June wedding, you see.'

'And not least because it meant no danger of sharing a honeymoon with these two.' Jack inclined his head toward the newly wed couple, who were laughing now and picking confetti off each other's bridal clothes. They both looked gloriously in love. 'I couldn't be happier for them, of course. Don't get me wrong. But when she suggested a double wedding and honeymoon … '

'I'm with you there, darling.' She made a face. 'God, that would have been a nightmare of epic proportions.'

'Ah, I love you for saying that. Under the circumstances.'

'I love you too, Jack.'

She turned her head and kissed him full on the lips. The sun danced warmly on her closed lids.

Crystal whispered in his ear, 'Mmm. Booking that isolated cottage on the moors was a brilliant idea. I want you all to myself on our honeymoon.' Her voice deepened seductively. 'Just you and me. Breakfast, lunch and dinner.'

He nuzzled her throat. 'I'm starving already.'

'The things I'm planning to do to you …'

Jack threw his head back with a bark of laughter. 'I can hardly wait, you saucy minx.' He squeezed her hard, then his expression sobered for a moment. 'So long as everything's okay, health-wise. I don't want to be responsible for a relapse.'

'You heard the consultant. No more hospital check-ups for at least another six months. The new liver is doing fine.' She sighed. 'I owe such a debt to the woman who died. Her poor family … '

'It was a road accident. Not your fault.'

'I still think about her.'

'Of course you do.'

'It's because of her death that I'm alive.'

'Then her generosity has given both of us a new chance.' His dark gaze met hers intently. 'You know, we never really discussed what happened. Those long hours when you were in surgery ... I kept remembering when the doctors told me about Beverley. How I'd lost her.' He stroked her cheek with one long finger, and she shivered at the intimate touch. 'I was going mad that day. I really thought I was going to lose you too.'

'No such luck.'

He grinned. 'Stuck with you forever, huh?'

'Afraid so.'

They kissed again, lost in the warmth of each other's arms, oblivious to the other wedding guests milling about them.

Then someone bumped them irreverently from behind.

'Hey, you two lovebirds. In public, remember? None of my business, of course, but maybe you should be saving all that smoochy stuff for after the wedding reception.'

It was Emma. She shook her head in mock disapproval as they surfaced from their long kiss, blinking in the sunshine as though they had only just woken up.

'What are you two like?'

Jack grinned but said nothing.

'Sorry.' Crystal pulled a contrite face. 'We totally forgot where we were. You know how it is.'

But Emma was not annoyed. 'I know exactly how it is,' she agreed, and kissed Crystal on the cheek, then hugged Jack. 'And I can't wait for your own big day. It's going to be amazing.'

'Thanks so much for agreeing to be my bridesmaid.'

Emma grinned. 'I wouldn't miss it for the world. Even if I do have to wear a huge green satin *thing*.'

'Hey, that dress looks amazing on you.'

'If you think looking like a gigantic green jelly is amazing, then yes.'

'Shut up.'

Rolling her eyes, Emma said nothing more on that subject, but her wry smile said it instead. She hated the green bridesmaid dress Crystal had chosen for her to wear, saying it was like choosing the wrong shade in a colouring book picture. But she was content to go with whatever the bride wanted, because it would be her special day.

My special day, Crystal thought happily, and hugged the incredible prospect to her heart.

Emma was right. Her wedding was going to be amazing, and not simply because she was going to become Jack's wife that day. She had made it through the lupus, she had made it through near liver failure, she had made it through the transplant and its aftermath, and she was not only alive but as close to healthy again as she could hope for. Healthy enough to get married and enjoy her very own honeymoon.

Now that's *special*, she told herself.

Jack had sunk his hands into the pockets of his expensive suit trousers, unable to look elegant even for a moment. Besides, Crystal knew that talk of weddings and dresses always bored him. He looked around restlessly. 'Where's Matthew?'

Emma gestured behind them, and they turned.

'Hi,' Matthew mouthed with a grin, and nodded to the sleeping bundle in his arms. 'I don't want to wake her.'

Emma's baby, Trudi, always seemed to sleep through public events. In fact, Crystal had never even heard her cry, except for a tiny cat-like wail she occasionally made before Emma picked her up for a feed.

'Awww, she's adorable.' Crystal looked at the baby's beautiful face with her pale features and long dark lashes, and her heart melted. She looked at Jack pleadingly. 'Can we? Please?'

'I told you,' Jack said sternly, 'not until we're sure you're well enough. Like the doctor said, pregnancy can be stressful on the body.'

'Tell me about it.' Emma winked at them, though in fact she looked to be glowing with health since the birth. 'And not just pregnancy. The first few months after the birth can be a stressful time too. It calls for lots of cake and TLC, especially if you decide to breastfeed. Isn't that right, Matthew?'

'Yes, dear.'

They all laughed at Matthew's dutiful tone.

'You've got him well-trained already,' Crystal said appreciatively. 'And you're not even married yet. Talking of which, have you set a date yet?'

'Probably the week before Christmas, if we can wrangle it,' Emma said, smiling, her face filled with happiness. 'I love Christmas, it's my favourite time of year. I can't wait to plan the decorations for our reception. I have this vision of it in my mind, based on a gorgeous picture I saw in one of our colouring books. I'll wear red and gold, and so will my bridesmaids. There'll be baubles and tinsel and a huge tree … and lots and lots of Christmas cake.'

'Sounds lavish,' Crystal said.

'And Dad has promised to give me away,' Emma added shyly. 'It's good to be back on speaking terms with my parents. Even if they haven't been the best mum and dad in the world lately.'

Jack leant forward and kissed Emma on the cheek. 'Good luck with the preparations. We'll definitely both be there.'

'I'm counting on it,' Matthew said quietly, and glanced down at Trudi as the baby yawned delicately and began to stretch. He lowered his voice even more. 'Because I want you to be my best man. If that's okay?'

'Sure,' Jack whispered.

Both men stared enraptured at the baby as her blue eyes opened and she surveyed their faces with interest.

'Wow,' Jack mouthed, clearly smitten.

Crystal caught Emma's eyes over the men's bent heads. They smiled secretly at each other. It won't take long to persuade him, Crystal was thinking.

'And you, my friend, will be there too, forced to wear a slinky gold satin dress as one of my bridesmaids.' Emma grinned at Crystal's wide-eyed horror. 'Hey, not a single word of criticism. Is that understood?'

'Yes, ma'am.'

A shout from behind them made the baby stiffen, and Matthew cradled her protectively, looking round in annoyance.

It was the photographer.

He tapped Emma hurriedly on the shoulder, his expression harassed. 'Family of the bride and groom?'

She pointed at Crystal. 'You want her, not me.'

'Family?' he repeated, turning to her.

Crystal nodded, then gasped at the man in sudden realisation. 'Wedding photos.' She grabbed Jack by the arm. 'Quick, Mum's going to kill me. I completely forgot. We were meant to gather for family photos after the ceremony finished. She must be waiting for us.'

Matthew looked up at Emma, also worried. 'That's us too. Come on, we'd better get over there.'

Crystal almost ran into the small but pretty garden at the back of the Register Office where they had said photographs could be taken. If she was too late …

But Fiona was far from angry, she saw with relief. In fact, she was busy handing out small woven bags containing colouring book and pencils to all the guests she could find.

'You'll really enjoy colouring in the pictures,' her mum was telling one old lady, a neighbour of theirs. The old lady cupped a hand to her ear, and Fiona shouted, 'Colouring. It's a *colouring* book. Yes, that's right. For colouring in pictures. We have a colouring book club that meets every few weeks. You'd be really welcome … '

Then she saw Crystal and turned, smiling broadly.

'Oh, sweetheart. Wasn't it a lovely ceremony? Of course, I would have preferred a church wedding, but … It was still lovely.'

'Mum, you look stunning.'

And Fiona really did look stunning. She was wearing an embroidered cream wedding dress that clung at the hips and flared into tulle at the knees, with a boldly plunging neckline. She had chosen cream satin pumps to match. And a gorgeous cream, white and green bouquet that was perfect for a spring wedding.

'Thanks, love.'

'Honestly, it's a knockout dress. And Boris looks amazing too.' Crystal grinned at the bridegroom. 'Who could have foreseen he'd look like James Bond once you stuck him in a tux?'

Boris looked awkward, and smoothed down his black jacket. 'Hello, Crystal. Enjoy the wedding?'

'It made me cry.' She smiled, then added, 'Dad.'

'Don't you dare Dad me.' He was looking anywhere but at her, a hard flush in his cheeks. He ran a tattooed hand over his shaven head. 'I'm Boris, you hear me? Just plain Boris.'

'Nothing plain about you,' Fiona said, and linked her arm with his, a satisfied expression on her face.

'Humph,' he said, making a face. But it was obvious he was secretly pleased. 'Your daughter's right about one thing though, Fifi,' he added gruffly, looking Fiona up and down with a piratical twinkle in his eye. 'You're a knockout in that dress.'

'Well, you only get married twice,' Fiona said flippantly. She glanced at her new husband with a knowing wink. 'Hopefully not more than twice though. Assuming you don't annoy me too much.'

'Don't bet on it,' Boris growled, but then spoilt it by grinning round at them all.

The photographer clapped his hands, sounding on the verge of hysteria. 'Positions, please. Family only in this shot.'

Matthew came to stand beside his dad, Emma proudly

by his side, with baby Trudi in her arms, wide-awake and gurgling. They might not be getting married until Christmas, but the three of them already made a perfect family unit, Crystal realised, her eyes filling with tears at the intimate glance Matthew and Emma shared over the baby's head.

And it was good to know Emma was back on friendly terms with both her parents, now they had realised what idiots they had been for shutting their daughter out of their life over one mistake.

The forecast last night had been for showers. But oh, she thought, what a beautiful day it was turning out to be.

'That's right,' Fiona said, then nudged her husband. 'Oh look, Boris, the baby's pretty as a picture today.'

'Better watch out Fiona doesn't try to colour her in,' Boris muttered to Emma and his son.

'I heard that,' Fiona said tartly.

Boris grinned.

'And you need to stand here, love,' Fiona told Crystal, pointing to the sunny spot beside her. 'On my left.'

Jack tried to slip away, but Fiona caught him by the arm. 'Not so fast, lad. You're family too.'

'Sorry, there's no escape,' Crystal whispered in his ear as she drew him back into the family shot. 'You're one of us now.'

Jack turned to look down at her. His smile was for her alone. 'Good.' They linked hands, palms fitting together perfectly as though they had been made for each other. 'I wouldn't have it any other way.'

Printed in Great Britain
by Amazon